The Bargain

By Jo Maseberg

FIRESIDE LIBRARY

A Fireside Library Book

OGDEN PUBLICATIONS INC.

Topeka, Kansas

Published by Ogden Publications
1503 SW 42nd St., Topeka, Kansas 66609

For more information about
Ogden Publications titles,
or to place an order, call:
(Toll-free) 1-800-678-4883.

ISBN 0-941678-68-7
First printing February 2001
Printed and bound
in the United States of America

To my parents who inspired within me a love of the written word and who encouraged me to share my own words – may this be the first of many.

– Jo Maseberg

Chapter 1

"Thank you for your time; we'll let you know." The man behind the desk told Jenny before lifting his phone, signaling the end of the interview.

She nodded and rose, hearing the unspoken, "don't call us, we'll call you," that she knew so well. As she left the office, she heard the low drone of the man's voice as he called for the next candidate to be sent in.

She walked down the long hall to the elevators, pressed the down arrow and stepped back, waiting. Moments later, the elevator doors whooshed open, and another young woman in a suit stepped out. She held some papers tightly in one hand, and Jenny saw an application on top of the pile. No doubt she was the next one to be interviewed.

Jenny swallowed the tears that rose in her throat and nodded to the woman, saying softly, "Good luck." The nervous young woman's face broke into a small smile at the unexpected kindness, and Jenny felt better for making the effort.

Stepping into the elevator, Jenny pressed the button

for the ground floor. She glanced in the smudged mirror that encircled the elevator, as the doors swished shut.

In the mirror, she saw a young woman in a neat pinstripe suit and sensible dark stockings and heels. Warm, chocolate brown eyes looked at her from a fine-boned face. She smiled, and her small mouth showed a row of straight, white teeth between full lips. Her shoulder-length, brown hair, neatly held back from her face with a blue bow, shimmered. The fluorescent lights brought out red highlights in it.

The elevator door opened, interrupting her reverie. She stepped into the lobby of the skyscraper and walked rapidly to the glass door. She pushed it open and stepped outside, almost gasping as she felt the heat. Downtown Houston in the middle of the summer was a sauna. For a moment, she paused, blinking in the bright sunlight. Then she straightened her shoulders and moved quickly down the sidewalk toward the parking garage.

She hadn't gotten the job. She'd known that since the moment the man had smiled reassuringly and said, "Mrs. Cook, I know this is illegal, but how many children do you have, and what does your husband do to make a living?"

She could have refused to answer, but then the man would have only thought the worst. Besides, she had been taught to tell the truth, no matter how much it hurt. "I have a four-year-old son. My husband died last year. He was killed by a drunk driver."

Jenny did not add that he had been picking her parents up from the airport, and that she had lost all three that awful night. She bit back tears as she stepped into the parking garage and walked to where she had parked the dilapidated ten-year-old hatchback.

Unlocking the door, she slid into the seat and quickly rolled down the windows. Then she stuck the key into the ignition.

What am I going to do now? This job interview was my last hope.

Ever since Jenny had lost her job, she and Peter had been living hand to mouth. The last of the furniture had been sold to pay the rent on a tiny furnished apartment, but even that had only lasted a few months. The rent was due in a week, and Peter's day care would need more money on Monday. She had only the meager emergency fund left.

What will happen when I can't buy food anymore? How am I going to take care of Peter?

She had no one left to turn to. Her parents were gone, and so was David. David's dad had died years ago, and his mother was in a nursing home with Alzheimer's disease. Both she and David had been only children.

3

The Bargain

What about her grandfather? No, I couldn't go back, not after what I said ... but for Peter's sake?

He has a ranch and cattle. At least Peter would be cared for.

The words of the psalmist came to her, and she thought she understood the despair echoed in them. "My God, my God, why have You forsaken me? ... Do not be far from me, for trouble is near and there is no one to help."

She stared blankly at the windshield, the hopelessness of it all catching up with her.

"Father in Heaven, I need a miracle," she whispered softly. "Please, Lord, help Peter and me – help us."

Jenny continued praying as she started the engine and drove onto the street. It was three o'clock, and she had to pick Peter up. He hadn't been feeling well this morning, but she had to take him to the day-care center anyway. This job interview had meant too much to miss. The way things had gone, she could have stayed home, but she had to try.

Negotiating the narrow streets, she found her way back to the freeway. The air that rushed into the car was hot and humid with the acrid taste of exhaust to it, but she welcomed the breeze. The suit was much too warm, and she wished she could change into shorts and a shirt.

Soon she saw her exit and left the freeway for the quiet, tree-lined streets near the day care. Peter went to the Christian day-care facility her church had opened up a short time ago. It had been a true miracle that she had gotten him enrolled there – and for less money than she would pay anywhere else.

She pulled into the parking lot and stepped out of the car, taking the keys but not bothering to lock it. If someone wanted to steal it, they could be her guest. It would serve them right if it didn't make it out of sight of the building before breaking down.

As Jenny entered the neat, brick building, she welcomed the cold draft from the overhead vent. She paused at the water fountain and took a long drink before continuing down the hall to the last door on the left.

The large room contained a peaceful scene. Twenty children sat bent over long tables, carefully coloring pictures with total concentration. A pretty, young woman circled among them, peering over shoulders and speaking words of praise and encouragement. Looking up, she saw Jenny. Smiling, she tapped a young boy's shoulder. He raised his head, and then hopped out of his chair.

"Mommy!" He dropped his crayon and ran across the room to greet her.

Jenny knelt down and gave him a big hug. The little boy's tousled brown hair and eyes matched her own, but his face was almost an exact replica of his father's. She held him tight a moment longer than usual before releasing him.

The Bargain

"Mommy, I made a drawing of Noah an' his elephants!"

"You did? May I see it?"

"Yeah, I'll go get it."

Then he was off again. Jenny rose to her feet as the young woman came to meet her.

"How's class today, Trish?" Jenny asked.

"Exciting as ever!" Trish smiled. "How did the interview go?"

"Not so good." Jenny shook her head, watching as Peter paused to share advice with a friend.

"I'm praying for you."

"Thank you." Jenny smiled. "We'll survive, somehow. With the Lord's help, we'll make out."

"I know." Trish nodded before changing the subject. "Peter was a little droopy this morning, but he was fine after an hour or so. I think he was just bothered by the heat. It never did cool down last night."

"I know." Jenny pushed back a stray strand of limp hair. "It's a real scorcher out there."

Peter came up, and the women ended their conversation. Jenny tied his shoe and took the small bag of clean clothes off the rack in the hall before taking his hand.

"You ready to go, fella?"

"Sure, Mommy. Can we have ice cream for a snack?"

Jenny mentally counted the change in her purse before making a quick decision. "Yup! We'll stop at the ice-cream store on the way home. How's that?"

"Yummy!" He rubbed his stomach and grinned up at her. The look in his eyes displayed infinite trust in her to make things work out all right. She smiled back, then braced herself as they pushed the outer door open and stepped outside.

An hour later, Jenny unlocked the door to their apartment, letting Peter go ahead of her into the stuffy room.

"Come on, kiddo, let's wash those sticky hands before you put them someplace Mommy doesn't want to clean up."

She helped him onto a chair in front of the tiny kitchen sink and turned the tap water on, making a game of splashing the water around – getting his hands clean in the process.

"All right, there you go." She helped him down and dried his hands and arms. "I'll open some windows and see if we can get a breeze."

He ran off toward his toys in the corner, and she pried the narrow, old-fashioned windows open and turned on the fans that sat in front of them. Drenched in sweat, she moved to the bedroom and decided on a shower. At least the lack of hot water wouldn't bother her.

Jenny felt much better after the cool shower. She dried off and dressed in a pair of white walking shorts and an airy, short-sleeved shirt. She was running a comb through her hair when she opened the bathroom door and heard Peter say, "Do you wanna talk to Mommy?"

Talk to Mommy? She hadn't heard the phone ring. Hurrying across the room, she took the receiver Peter offered.

"Hello?" she asked, smiling at Peter and tweaking his nose gently.

"Jenny Cook?" The man's voice was friendly but unfamiliar.

"This is she."

"Ma'am, this is Jon Carlisle, your grandfather's attorney, and I'm afraid I've got some bad news."

"Yes?" What could possibly be worse than losing David?

"Your grandfather, Peter Riley, died yesterday."

"Grandfather's dead?" She groped for the chair behind her and sat down.

"Yes'm. His neighbor found him. He died in his sleep sometime last night.

"It would be nice if you could make it to the funeral. It'll be in three days, on Monday."

"I ..."

He hurried on. "After the funeral, we'll be reading the will, and that might interest you." The phone crackled and she missed what he said after that.

"Pardon?"

"Ma'am, he left you the ranch," the man said loudly. The ranch? "I'll – I'll be there," she said faintly.

"Good. I'm Jon Carlisle, and I'll meet you at ..."

"Wait, let me get some paper and a pen." Hurriedly, she scribbled down the directions he gave her. Then he bid her goodbye and hung up.

Setting the receiver gently back into its cradle, Jenny stared at the piece of paper in her hands, stunned. Grandfather's dead. ... Was this the way God answered her plea for help? No, God did not take pleasure in the death of His children. Grandfather had been old, very old. Yet, to lose the only family she had left ...

Tears pooled in her eyes, and she began to sob uncontrollably. First David and her parents, and now this. What if ... what if I die? What would happen to Peter? He's such a little boy.

She felt Peter's arm around her neck and his small hand patting her back.

"It's OK, Mommy," he said softly. "You'll be OK."

She choked back the tears and tried to smile. "I know."

"It's OK to miss Daddy," Peter spoke reassuringly. "I do too."

"It's – it's not that, not really. The call was from a lawyer. He called to tell me something important."

She offered her lap, and Peter climbed up. How do I tell him the awful truth?

"Do you remember, in the photo album, the picture of

The Bargain

Mommy when she was a little girl, riding a horse?"

Peter nodded.

"Remember how I told you that the man standing next to the horse was my Grandpa? Well, Grandpa owned a ranch. A ranch is sort of like a farm, only with cows instead of crops."

"Cows? Like that give milk?"

"Yeah. Sort of like that. Well, Grandpa was an old man, and yesterday – yesterday he died."

"Will he go to Heaven an' be with Jesus, like Grandpa Sam?" Peter asked.

"I think so." Jenny smiled reassuringly before continuing, "Grandpa lived in Nebraska, and the man who called wants me to go to the funeral. He also told me that Grandpa had given you and me the ranch."

"Ranch? With the cows?"

"Yes. I – I think we'll be going to live there."

The little boy smiled and hopped down off her lap, relieved. There was a picture in one of his books that had cows in it.

Jenny watched as he trotted off. She had been Peter's age when she first met Grandpa. He had been a wonderful man, always happy. He had shown her the world on the ranch, the round sky overhead and the sea of grass beneath. They had spent long, lazy days in a rowboat fishing on the lake. He had taught her how to ride horses and find newborn kittens.

Then everything had changed. They had grown so far

apart in recent years. When her family moved south, the visits home to the old ranch had become fewer. Then they did not return at all. Why did we never go back? Why did we let it end like this?

Jenny shook her head and tried to clear the cobwebs from her mind. The funeral was Monday, and it was a thousand miles away. If she was going to get there in time, she would have to pack right away.

"Thank you, God, for giving me somewhere to go. I just ... Help me to accept Your will in this matter."

Chapter 2

Dusk filtered through the small window above the kitchen sink, but there was no respite from the heat. Jenny dried the last dish and emptied the dishwater from the sink. She dried her hands on the damp dishcloth before turning to the pile of clean silverware on the table. The long plastic container that she used to store bread in would work perfectly. She dumped the silverware into it and sealed the lid tight before getting another couple of packing boxes.

It felt good to have somewhere to go, but to have lost Grandfather? With a heavy heart, Jenny put a box on the table and packed the plates and cups, wrapping them in clean towels. She packed her glass bowls and the few things she hadn't sold at the garage sale last year in another box and slipped the silverware container on top.

She glanced across the room and saw that Peter had cried himself to sleep. He had been fretful ever since supper, when he had spilled water all over his favorite picture book. His hair hung limp, and she moved across the room and brushed the damp locks from his forehead. It was too hot, much too hot.

She had removed the top sheet and blanket from Peter's bed in the corner of the living room earlier and packed them. Now she lifted him from the floor onto the bed. Even the bottom sheet was no longer crisp and cool.

Oh, what she wouldn't give to get away from this heat.

"Tomorrow we're going north," she reminded herself. North. Even the word sounded cool and wonderful to her.

The refreshing thought helped renew her energy so she could finish packing. All that was left in the kitchen was the ice chest that she would fill with bottles of water in the morning. Other than that, only a few things in her bedroom remained to be packed.

She moved to her room and surveyed it. It seemed more barren now than ever, with the homey comforter and curtains removed. Her clothes were still in the battered chest of drawers, so she would start with them. She pulled a suitcase onto the bed and emptied the drawers into it neatly.

After zipping up the suitcase, she lugged it to the living room and piled it with boxes. She moved to the bookcase and knelt in front of it. The shelves were bowed under the weight of the books.

After David died, she had sold nearly everything

from their beautiful suburban home, but she hadn't been able to part with her books – her friends. The city could be the loneliest place on Earth, and each book had come to be a treasured friend, each with its own voice. One was the book David had given her the first year they were married, and another had been her mother's favorite as a girl. Jenny could almost hear her father's voice reading from Longfellow's poetry collection. Best of all was the thick Bible she had received for her tenth birthday. It never failed to give her comfort. Running her hands over the spines, she lifted those three out and put them in a box.

Her Bible would travel in her purse.

When she was done, she changed into a T-shirt and shorts before laying down on the lumpy bed. Wrapping her arms around the pillow, she faced another lonely night. There was a great emptiness inside her, as though a part of her was missing now that David was gone. Life had been so crazy since David died. She hadn't stopped missing him. But for Peter's sake, she had to be strong.

For Peter's sake. ... Was starting on a journey of more than a thousand miles in a worn-out car with no money the best thing she could do? A million things could happen between here and Nebraska. ...

No! She wouldn't start thinking like that. She would

put their lives in God's hands and trust Him to take care of them. He had provided so much; surely He wouldn't give up on them now.

"Father, thank you for providing us a place to go. Please help Peter and me get to Nebraska safely. Amen. Oh, and God, tell David that Peter and I are OK, but I miss him so much."

A quiet peace stole over her, but it was a long time before she could get to sleep.

Jenny awakened at five a.m., just before the alarm rang. For a moment, she lay still planning her day. Rising, she showered, braided her hair down the back and dressed in cool, white shorts and a blouse. She was fastening her sandals when Peter came in.

"Good morning, sweetie," she said cheerfully.

"Mornin', Mommy," he answered, noticing his clothes laid out on the bed.

"If you want to get dressed, I'll finish getting ready to go."

"OK."

A few minutes later, he was dressed in knit shorts and a shirt, and Jenny was tying his shoes. Then they picked up the dirty clothes and took the sheets off the beds, putting them in a garbage sack. After Jenny emptied the contents of the refrigerator into the ice chest, she unlocked the door, ready to take the boxes to the car.

Opening the door, she looked out at the quiet parking

lot. Birds chattered, and already the day was hot. Putting the keys in her pocket, she picked up the first box. She was thankful they were on the ground floor. Seven boxes, the ice chest, two suitcases and a sack filled the small car. She buckled Peter into the front seat and returned to the apartment for one last check.

She looked around the tiny, stifling rooms before closing the door one last time and locking it. She dropped her keys into an envelope and slipped it under the manager's door. Now they were ready to leave.

"Goodbye, city," she murmured, standing a moment longer before walking down the sidewalk to her car. There was no one left for her to depend on but God. Had Ruth felt this way, starting a long journey from her homeland with Naomi? "Father, help me," she prayed again.

She opened the door and slid into her seat, pushing the key into the ignition and buckling her seat belt.

"We goin' now, Mommy?"

"Yes. You ready?"

He nodded, and she started the car, backing out of the parking lot into the street, deserted at this hour. They would have to buy gas, and maybe she would get some doughnuts to serve as a makeshift breakfast. Jenny smiled to herself as she pulled up at the intersection. Leaving town on two hundred dollars was either a very big act of faith, or the craziest thing she had ever done. Either way, God had opened a door for her and Peter in

Nebraska, and she knew she had to take it.

Two hours passed before they saw the end of Houston, and Jenny was more than relieved to see it go. They were on I-45 north to Dallas. A gospel station came in over the radio, but she didn't have much chance to listen. Peter asked questions about everything, and the morning passed quickly.

Around eleven they found a rest stop where they could eat sandwiches for lunch, then they got back on the road again. After lunch, the road seemed a lot longer. Jenny wished she could stop, but she kept driving, and much to her relief they reached Oklahoma City at five.

It was six-thirty when they got to Perry, Okla., and it was a welcome sight. They found a motel, got a room, then had supper at McDonald's. It was still early when Jenny put her nightgown on, but she was asleep when her head hit the pillow. If today was anything to go by, tomorrow was going to be grueling.

Peter crawled down out of bed, as his mother's breathing evened out, and knelt on the floor. She had forgotten to hear him say his prayers. God was listening, though, and He was the one who mattered. Peter would say them by himself.

"Now I lay me down to sleep, pray the Lord my soul to keep, guide me safely through the night, wake me with the morning light. In Jesus' name, Amen." He hopped up, ready to crawl back into bed, then bowed his head once more. "Oh yeah, an' God, please bless Mommy. Amen."

Returning to bed, he curled up, tired, but looking forward to the next day. They would get there, Mommy said. He was eager to see what there was like. As he drifted off to sleep, he shivered. The noisy air conditioner under the window had chilled the room, and for the first night in a long time, Peter slept with the blankets on.

Jenny's alarm clock went off at five-thirty, and she was up shortly after, refreshed and ready to go. At six they were on the road, headed north. The sun was up, casting long shadows over the land. They passed through Kansas and ate lunch in York, Neb., before getting on the interstate headed west. Four hours later, they were in Ogallala.

Jenny left the interstate and drove slowly through town. At four o'clock on Sunday afternoon, it was a sleepy little town. She passed houses with great trees overhead and yards with dogs and small children playing. The smell of backyard barbecues drifted through the open windows, reminding her that this was a cattle town, first with the Texas trail herds and now with the surrounding ranches. It was ironic that she, a Texan, would be ranching near here.

The Bargain

The street out of town was quiet, residential, and one-way. Curving around, it suddenly faced the highway. Jenny came to a halt in front of the stop sign and gazed ahead. A large motor home pulling a small jeep was coming down the hill into town, and she watched as it passed. It must have come from Lake McConaughy, a big lake a few miles north of town.

She pulled onto the two-lane road out of town, quickly leaving Ogallala behind. She turned west onto the highway to Cottonwood. Just a little while longer and they would be at the end of the trip. Jenny smiled and turned on the radio. The only station she could get was one that had country music. She rarely listened to that type of music. Maybe this was another sign that she had entered a whole new world. Grinning, she listened to the lyrics of the song –

"On the road again, I just can't wait to get on the road again, I ..."

They drove into Cottonwood, or rather, through it, an hour later. Realizing she had gone too far, Jenny turned south onto the highway leading to the North Platte river. She pulled off the highway before the bridge crossed the river and unbuckled her seat belt. She got out of the car. Peter followed suit, and she said a quick prayer of thanks for safe passage. Then she joined Peter, who was looking at the river. She was incredibly tired, but she had never been happier to get somewhere.

In the shade of tall trees, she walked around, stretching her legs. It felt good to be out of the car. For a moment, she felt that she wouldn't mind at all if she never had to get in again. They spent half an hour stretching and playing, until the sky clouded over and thunder rumbled. They got back in the car and drove back to town. The two ate supper before getting a room at the small motel.

Jenny grabbed the suitcases and ran for the shelter of the room as the first drops of rain fell. Inside, she fished Peter's coloring book and crayons from the smaller suitcase and set him to work at the tiny table. Then she opened the big one. Tomorrow was the funeral, and she needed to see how many wrinkles her good black dress had accumulated during the long trip north.

Shaking it out, she was pleased to see it didn't look too bad. It was a plain dress with short sleeves and a straight skirt that hit below her knees. It zipped up the back. She held it up before hanging it on the clothes rod. The last time she had worn this was at David's and her parents' funerals.

Blotting the memory from her mind, she remembered the way they used to be: David, tossing Peter high on his shoulders at the zoo; Mom, basting the turkey for Christmas dinner; and Dad, getting the family Bible down for morning devotions. There had been bad times too, but those only made the good times better.

She thanked God for having had her family as long as she did. She was not bitter about the loss, just sad. She knew that her family was safe with God, but she missed them, and she always would.

Now she must look ahead. She had a son to raise and a ranch to learn about. With God's help, she would manage. She had to.

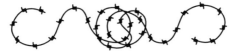

They slept in until seven the next morning. Before her shower, she gave Peter a bath. Then he played while she got ready for the day. Emerging from the bathroom, she saw that Peter had found the sack with his wooden blocks in it.

"That's quite a city you've built," she commented, separating her hair with the comb.

"Yup. See, it's got twenty hundred people in it, an' they live here, an' here, an' over there. That's a store." He pointed.

"And what's that?" she asked.

"That's a church."

"That's a good city." She smiled and ruffled his hair as she returned to the bathroom for a rubber band to snap on the end of her French braid. After tying a black chiffon bow around her braid, she ran a brush through Peter's hair and sorted out his nice pants and shirt. They were almost too small, but they would do for today.

After they dressed, Jenny packed the suitcase. Tonight they would be home. Home ... it had a nice sound. After reloading the car, they drove to the cafe where they were to meet the lawyer for breakfast. As they got out of the car, a tall, older man with white hair and a warm smile approached.

"Mrs. Cook? I'm Jon Carlisle. We spoke on the phone."

Chapter 3

The morning passed in a blur. At the funeral, Jenny met her grandfather's neighbors and friends, but they became just a sea of faces. Peter had clung close to her, and they comforted each other.

Now she found herself standing alone beside the grave. The morning was gone and with it, the people. Peter was asleep in the car, and she knew she should go check on him.

She was standing in the small cemetery on the tall, grass-covered hill, thinking how peaceful it was. The wind was from the west, and it felt good as it blew across her face. The sun was high in the sky, blindingly bright and warm. It was a beautiful day, perfect for a picnic, but instead she had attended a funeral. She knew she had to leave, but not yet. Just one more moment.

She gazed at the mound of dirt and sod in front of her, and then at the small plaque in the earth. Peter J. Riley, Gone Home, it said. Two dates were below it, but that was all. It was what he had wished, but it said nothing of the man.

The Bargain

"Well, Peter J. Riley," she spoke softly, "if you were here, you'd ask me why I'm crying. I've no excuse, you'd say, and you'd be right. You're in God's hands now, and I ..." She broke off, the familiar lump in her throat signaling the tears that blurred her vision. She knelt down by the grave, scooping up a handful of the cool, dark earth. Tears spilled from her eyes as she looked up.

"I'm going to miss you, Grandpa, but I won't forget you. ... I'm going to teach my son what you taught me, and I'm going to tell him all about you. ... Oh, Grandpa, how am I going to manage?"

Peter sat on the ground by the car, waiting. The grasshoppers were making noise, hopping away from him when he moved, and he liked to watch them. He wished Mommy would hurry up. He squinted. The sun was so bright! Then a shadow fell over him, and he glanced up. A tall man was kneeling down in front of him.

"Hi there," the man said in a friendly voice. He was wearing a big cowboy hat, the straw kind. Brown hair curled out from underneath, and Peter decided that someday he would have a hat like that.

"Hi," Peter said.

"What're you doin' here all by yourself?" the man

asked gently, one knee in the grass, his boot toes scrunched up.

"Waitin' on Mommy."

"She's your Mom?" He gestured to the lone figure on the hill.

"Yeah."

"That sun bothering you?" the man asked, as the sun hit Peter in the face.

"Kinda." Peter squinted.

"Just a minute, I have something that might help." He rose and moved away, walking to a dusty blue pickup parked beyond the car. He opened the door, reached in and took something off the dash. When he returned, Peter saw he held a cap. Carefully the man tightened the back strap, then he placed it firmly on Peter's head. The bill created instant shade, and Peter grinned appreciatively.

"Thanks! Thanks a lot, mister."

"Call me Mike. What's your name?"

"Peter."

"It's nice to meet you, Peter." Mike held out a hand, shaking Peter's small one.

Peter looked surprised, but returned the clasp. He was really a cute kid, Mike thought. His mother had done a good job raising him, something that was no doubt very difficult after she had lost her husband. He glanced up the hill at the small figure with her back to them. The sun glanced off her head, and tiny red glimmers appeared in the brown hair. He remembered what he'd seen of her at the funeral, recalling the petite frame and the delicate face with the sorrow etched across it.

"Come on, Peter." Mike glanced down at his small friend. "Let's go see if your mom's ready to go."

Peter clambered to his feet, and they walked up the hill. Mike noted the woman's straight back as he approached her. He remembered that Peter Riley, his good friend and close neighbor, had the same erect posture, the same shade of hair. She looked much like her grandfather, Mike saw. Would she stay at the ranch, though, as her grandfather had wished?

Michael Snow had his own ranch. It bordered Peter Riley's. The two neighbors had worked together the last few years, caring for both ranches' cattle herds. Mike had come to know and like his neighbor, and he had felt as though his own grandfather had died when he had found Peter Riley's body.

"Ma'am?"

The soft voice came from behind Jenny, and she turned, allowing the dirt to trickle through her fingers.

A man was standing there, holding Peter by the hand. He was tall, over six feet she guessed. He had a strong face, browned by the sun, but it was strangely gentle as well. Or maybe it was his eyes – they were kind, caring, tender. Their shade of brown reminded her of dark chocolate. Dressed in blue jeans and a white shirt with a string tie, he was good looking in a rugged way.

"Yes?" She asked.

"I'll show you the way back to the ranch, whenever you're ready to go."

"Thank you." She nodded and turned back to the grave. For a moment, she was silent, letting the last of the earth be blown by the wind from her hand. Then she turned back.

"I'm ready now, if you are." Jenny said. "Thank you for waiting so long." She smiled wearily.

"I understand, ma'am," he said quietly.

Looking into the dark brown eyes, she knew that he truly did. There was a sadness in him, and she felt that his expression mirrored her own.

"Thank you." Her lips emitted the barest whisper of sound, but he heard.

He nodded, relinquishing Peter's small hand, and the strange spell of shared pain was gone. She found herself longing to regain the moment, but he was speaking again.

"I'll lead out, and you just follow. I'll keep a close watch so I don't lose you. The roads are tricky if you don't know them – and sometimes if you do." He grinned.

"All right." She nodded and they walked back to their vehicles.

The man got into the truck and started the engine. Waiting until she had started her car, he backed out and led her north on the desolate road into the Sand Hills.

They were on a one-way gravel lane, and if she remembered correctly it was an hour's drive to the ranch.

Jenny glanced at Peter and saw he was settled comfortably in the seat, looking out the window. She glanced ahead again and had to concede that the country was worth looking at. The rugged, windblown hills were shaped like dunes in a desert, covered in long, gray-green grass that blew in the wind like the waves on the sea.

Her black dress was soaking wet in the heat from the sun streaming through the window. Jenny shifted in her seat, trying to escape the merciless rays, but it was no use. She tried to concentrate on something else. The man's blue truck was leaving a long trail of dust behind it as it sped along the road. Who was this man? She felt as though she had known him a long time.

"And yet I don't even know his name," she muttered to herself.

"Who's name, Mommy?" Peter piped up.

"That man's."

"Oh. His name is Mike." Peter informed her proudly. "An' he gave me this hat, to keep the sun out of my eyes."

Jenny glanced sideways and saw the hat. It was deep red with the name of an animal clinic embroidered on it. She smiled and nodded before turning her attention back to the road. It was a big cap for such a little boy. It came to just above his eyebrows. But it did help keep the sun out of his eyes. She would have to remember to thank Mike.

Mike – the name suited him, she decided. Braking gently for a sharp curve, she took a better look at the road. It would definitely not be something she would want to attempt if it were raining or snowing. And for the next twenty minutes, she was forced to concentrate solely on driving. They passed a tall, lone pine tree standing next to the road on the top of a long hill, then the gravel gave way to a black top road barely one lane wide.

The car finally quit shaking, and Jenny was thankful. Then she glanced at the sides of the road. There were no shoulders. Instead, she noticed, there were ditches on both sides, ranging anywhere from ten to twenty feet straight down. There were barbed wire fences at the bottom.

She concentrated on her driving, trying to ignore the threat to life and limb only feet away. The road went steeply down, then swooped up another long hill, just like a roller coaster. Clinging to the steering wheel, Jenny wondered how anyone could stand to live on a road like this. Could she?

"Mommy?" Peter said, with an urgent sound in his voice.

"What?"

" I ... I feel really sick."

She stepped on the brake and the car lurched to a

stop. Jenny managed to get him unbuckled and to the side of the road before he lost his dinner.

A long half-hour later, Jenny pulled into the ranch yard and parked next to Mike's pickup, in front of the long, low garage. She switched the key off and sat still a moment, glancing sideways at Peter. He was pale, gulping fresh air. But other than that, he seemed to be doing all right.

She unfastened her seat belt and got out of the car, taking a quick look around. They had driven in past a tall red and white barn that had a maze of corrals to the east. Looking west, she saw that the house was just as she remembered it, surrounded by cottonwood and elm trees. The lawn needed a trim, but it was lush and green. The old house itself was two stories high with weathered white siding and neat blue trim. Two rocking lawn chairs sat comfortably under a tree in the shade, and a porch swing beckoned on the wide front porch. One sidewalk led to the front porch, and another led around the house to the back door. The house faced south, looking out across the meadow.

The meadow stretched out, a grass carpet with the sparkling blue waters of the twin ponds shining in its center. At the edge of one were four spreading willow trees. A Russian olive tree stood south of the house, its silver-white leaves waving in the breeze. What really caught her attention, however, were the huge, golden haystacks randomly scattered around the meadow; long shadows stretched behind them. A hawk sat on the rounded top of one stack, surveying his kingdom. Long beaked curlews scurried across the meadow in search of insects, and ducks squabbled. Surrounded by the hills, the meadow was an oasis of life in a seemingly barren land.

The car door slammed and she almost jumped. Peter was walking slowly around the front of the car to stand by her side. Mike led the way to the house, opening the back door without unlocking it. Stepping aside, he ushered them into the coolness of the closed porch. It held a sink, a coat rack along one wall, a washer and dryer, a freezer, and a door to the kitchen. They stepped into the kitchen, and Jenny blinked, as her eyes adjusted to the light. Windows on the south wall let the afternoon sunlight stream in. Mike stepped over and cranked them open, letting the breeze in.

"I watered the plants yesterday, so they'll be all right for a while. I washed the sheets and tried to clean up a bit. The cat food is on the porch. You need to feed them half the coffee can full every morning. You can feed them your table scraps as well." Mike checked things off on his fingers.

"Cats?"

"The rascals are all down for their afternoon siestas,

aren't they?" He chuckled. "Usually they camp on the doorstep, all ten of them. They're not house cats, so don't worry about leaving them out. They just need fresh water in the bowl on the sidewalk each morning along with their food."

"All right." Jenny nodded. Peter had brightened up when he heard that he had ten pets.

"The food in the fridge is good – I tossed out the leftovers yesterday. If you can't find something, call me." He grabbed a tablet and pencil from the stand under the telephone and scribbled a number on it. "I'm your closest neighbor – I live a mile up the road. Ben Thomson and his wife, Anna, live south about five miles, at the far end of your summer range. Here's their number." He wrote it below his, along with their names.

"They were at the funeral, weren't they?" Jenny asked, looking at the names.

"Yeah. The older couple."

"Uhm, wasn't everyone older?" Jenny asked delicately.

Mike laughed. "I guess they were."

"Anna was the nice lady that hugged me, right? With the really tall husband?"

"Yeah, that's them. They're good people."

"So, if I need help, call?" She asked lightly.

"Sure. I may not be in all the time, but keep callin' and you'll catch me."

"All right."

"I'd better be going now." He turned back to the door. "Looks like rain, and you'll want to get settled in."

"Thank you, for everything."

"No problem." He grinned, and she couldn't help smiling back. "Will you two be OK?"

"Sure." She nodded.

"Bye then. Take care, Peter." Mike chucked him lightly under the chin and headed out the door. Jenny followed and stood in the doorway as his truck roared to life and he backed out of the drive. He waved, and she felt very alone as his truck disappeared onto the road.

She saw that Peter looked as lost as she felt. Suddenly they were all alone, the closest person a mile away. How were they going to do this? She said a quick prayer and smiled at Peter.

"Why don't we go unpack the car before it rains? Then we can find something to eat."

He nodded and followed as she left the house. In the west, dark clouds rolled in; lightning darted like a snake's tongue through the clouds. The storm was far enough away that they couldn't hear the answering rumble of thunder. With a shiver, Jenny realized that the wind had freshened before the storm. She rubbed her arms, reaching for the suitcases.

Chapter 4

A few minutes later, Jenny let the screen door slam shut behind her as she set the last box in the kitchen. The thunder rolled, and she jumped. Rain spattered against the windows, changing quickly into a steady beat. Mentally calming herself, Jenny glanced at her watch – four o'clock. She had given Peter a peanut butter and jelly sandwich earlier, but she hadn't eaten anything. Now she was ravenous.

First, I'll do something with my belongings, she thought. The packing boxes were stacked on the kitchen floor, on stools and on the breakfast bar. The ice chest was in front of the refrigerator, and Jenny decided to start with it. Opening it, she lifted out a dripping sack of ice and quickly carried it to the sink, one hand underneath to catch the drips. She dropped it into the bottom of the deep double sink, and she returned to the refrigerator and began filling the top shelf with bottles of water. When she was done, she put the ice chest on the porch under the coat rack.

Next came the boxes of kitchen utensils. Her two

37

pans joined a multitude of copper-bottom kettles that hung above the island on a rustic wooden rack. Her dishes fit easily into spacious cupboards.

Stashing the boxes on the porch, Jenny returned to the kitchen. She was bending to pick up another box when she remembered Peter. Where was he? She hadn't seen him since before the storm started.

"Peter?" she yelled, standing up, the box forgotten at her feet.

Silence. Hurrying to the door that separated the living room from the kitchen, she glanced quickly around the room. No Peter. She called again, flinging doors open. The dining room, a bathroom and a den revealed no one.

Anxiously, she took the stairs two at a time to the second floor. Here she faced a long hall and five more doors, all closed.

"Peter!" she yelled, opening the door to a large linen closet. Nothing.

Across the hall, she found a bathroom. The next two rooms were bedrooms, empty of life. Reaching for the last door, she suddenly became very scared. The hall ended in a set of glass doors that opened onto a balcony, and the doors were open. The carpet was wet at the edge, and she feared the worst. Stepping out into the downpour, she stared at the ground below, unmindful of the cold rain. Jenny felt only relief when she didn't see Peter.

Retreating into the house, she shut the doors firmly and latched the hook at the top to lock them. She saw that the last door was open a crack. She pushed it open, then took a ragged breath. Peter was safe. He turned to face her.

"Mommy, come see," Peter said from his place on the window seat.

Slowly she crossed the floor, never taking her eyes off his small form. He scooted over and made room for her to sit. She looked out at the wet branches of a tree. Beyond it, she saw the meadow and the lakes.

"Pretty, huh?" Peter asked, his face pressed against the glass.

"Yes, it is," she said shakily.

Peter turned from the window, alerted by the unnatural sound of her voice.

"What's wrong, Mommy?" he asked, with a concerned look in his eyes.

"I – I couldn't find you, and you didn't answer when I called. I was worried."

"I'm OK," he assured her.

"I know." Jenny tried to smile, for Peter's sake. "But I was really worried. I want you to tell me next time you plan to disappear. OK?"

"OK." Peter nodded. "But I wanted to see what our house was like. Isn't this a pretty room?"

For the first time, she looked around. This was the master bedroom, on the southwest corner of the house.

They were sitting in the wide bay window on the south wall, a matching seat was on the west wall. The antique, cherry four-poster was centered on the north wall, facing the windows. A night stand with a telephone and a lamp sat to one side, with the closet door on the other. A tall bureau and a heavy desk and chair were the only other pieces of furniture. Thick blue carpet set off the cornflowers in the delicate, floral wallpaper.

"It's very pretty," she agreed.

"Will it be yours?" Peter asked.

"If you don't want it." She grinned.

"No. It looks like a girl's room," he said so seriously that she almost laughed.

"All right," she conceded, repressing a smile. "Have you chosen a room yet?"

"No."

"Well, why don't we go look? Then you can unpack your things."

They moved back into the hall and opened the door opposite the master bedroom. This room had a double bed, a dresser and a full-length mirror. The closet was empty, as were the dresser drawers. The carpet was the same blue as the other room, but the walls were plain white.

"I like this one." Peter decided.

"All right. This one it is," she agreed. "But I want to see the rest of the house before I bring the boxes up, OK?"

"Sure."

They went back to the hall and peeked in the next room. A bed, dresser and night stand were in this room. There were also clothes in the closet and shoes on the floor. Had her grandfather been staying in here instead of in the master bedroom?

She didn't have time to think about that. Peter was into the next door – the linen closet. It was as big as her bedroom in the apartment had been, and it was stocked with a variety of things, from sheets and towels to yarn and lengths of fabric. They shut the door and stepped across the hall to the big bathroom. It was connected to the master bedroom through the large walk-in closet.

"Mommy, I could go swimming in the tub." Peter laughed.

"It sure looks that way, doesn't it." She gazed at the big bathtub under the window. It would be wonderful for long soaks. After a quick glance around, she followed Peter back into the hall and down the wide stairs to the living room.

At the bottom of the stairs, she found herself facing the heavy, oak front door. On impulse, she opened it and looked out the screen door at the rain dripping off the edge of the porch roof. The whole world was a soggy, wonderfully wet place. The first mad rush of drops had become a steady shower. Even the lightning had abated somewhat. Stepping back into the house, Jenny left the door open to the cool breeze and the smell of the rain, so unlike anything she had known in Texas.

She made a trip to the kitchen and located the promised carton. She toted Peter's box upstairs to his room and returned to haul up the suitcases and the rest of the boxes. By the time she finished, she was wishing for a house with only one level. There were too many stairs for comfort.

Setting the last box down in the linen closet, she collapsed on the floor beside it, breathing hard. Finally she opened it and began unpacking towels and sheets. Another box held the big comforter from her bed, but she didn't need it yet. Placing the box on a shelf, without unpacking it, she went to find Peter.

He was arranging stuffed animals on his bed, and she saw the rest of his belongings scattered about the room.

"You ready for something to eat?" she asked, glancing at her watch. "It's after five."

"Yeah!" he said enthusiastically. "I'm hungry."

They trooped back to the kitchen, now empty of boxes. Digging in the refrigerator, Jenny found a bottle of chocolate sauce. If there was that ... Playing a hunch, she peered in the freezer. Yep, ice cream. Pulling out the carton of vanilla, she got out two bowls and spoons and a scoop. They each had a bowl, shivering deliciously as it slid in icy paths to their stomachs.

"Mmm." Peter licked the last drop from his spoon. "That was good."

"You're right about that."

Jenny pushed her bowl away, ready for something a little more substantial. She hadn't had much to eat all day. At breakfast, she'd been too nervous and at lunch, overwhelmed. Now she dug the makings for two sandwiches out of the refrigerator and quickly put them together.

"Here, have a sandwich, kiddo." She handed one to Peter and took the other. They ate silently, each lost in thought.

After they ate, she rinsed the dishes and stacked them in the sink. Peter returned to his room, and she let him go, satisfied that he was safe and at ease in his new surroundings.

Jenny wandered through the house again, looking over the place that had suddenly become her home. It was a big, beautiful house. It was older, she admitted, but it was like nothing she would ever have again. No matter how hard it was going to be to learn to run the ranch, God obviously wanted her here.

"Thank you," she whispered. She wandered from the kitchen into the dining room. There was a beautiful wood floor in here. The dark cherry table glistened in the gray light from the wall of windows to the north. Twelve chairs sat around it. A matching hutch against one wall held the good china, and Jenny glanced at her grandmother's dishes inside. This, she knew, had been her grandmother's favorite room, and Jenny almost felt her presence – in the lace curtains, the dainty wallpaper and the cut-glass light fixtures.

"I have to stay," she murmured to herself. "How could I leave all this?"

The room did not answer, and she watched the rain fall outside in the gathering darkness. She returned to the den in search of a book to read aloud to Peter before bed.

It was more of a library than a den. She felt her grandfather's spirit there the same way she felt her grandmother's in the dining room. Floor to ceiling bookcases lined the walls. A thick rag rug covered most of the floor. Two large chairs sat side by side in front of the tall, narrow windows. She had learned a love of books from her grandfather in this very room. She was glad to see that it hadn't changed. He had kept a shelf full of children's storybooks, and now she searched through them, finding one that Peter was sure to like. Switching off the light, she made sure everything was ready for the night before she went upstairs.

Peter was already in his pajamas, sitting on the bed with his stuffed rabbit. The rabbit was having a lively discussion with a toy bear on the end of the bed about just what a ranch was.

"Well, I still think a ranch should have sun. Look at this rain!" Peter was saying for the rabbit. Jenny took the bear and spoke in a gruff voice.

"There will be sun, bright and early tomorrow morning. But you have to go to sleep first."

"Sleep? Now?" Peter asked, forgetting the rabbit.
"Not yet, silly. Right after we read this book." She
held it up, and he looked at its worn cover skeptically.
"Only if it's long," he bargained.
"Oh, I wouldn't worry about that." Jenny sat cross-
legged on the end of the bed and opened the book.

Peter was nearly asleep when she finished. He said
his prayers, and then she tucked the sheet up around
his shoulders. Kissing him gently, she turned quietly to
leave the room.
"Mommy?" he asked softly.
"Hmm?"
"Can we stay here forever?"
"Not that long," she said in the darkness, "but a long,
long time."
"I'd like that."
"So would I." She bent over and kissed his cheek
again. "You get some sleep now, OK? We can see more
tomorrow when the sun's shining."
He nodded off, and she went out, leaving the door
open. She switched the night light in the hall on before
she entered her room. Her room – she was truly home
at last.
She changed into pajamas and pulled down the fluffy
comforter. She glanced at the clock and made sure the

alarm was set before crawling into the clean, sweet-smelling sheets. Relaxing, she let her guard slip.

"Oh David, why aren't you here?" she asked the darkness. "Why aren't you here with me now, beside me, holding me?"

"Because you're gone," she answered herself. "Because you're gone, and you'll never be here again."

The dull ache that had not left her since the moment he died sharpened, and she turned over, her eyes shut against the pain. At least there were no memories of him in this house, on this ranch. Jenny would never look at the sink and recall him doing dishes there, would never remember him in a hundred little places when she least expected it. Would it be easier, though, to forget? No, she would never forget. She just had to let the memories grow old, and maybe some day they would fade away. That's what she told herself, but in her heart of hearts, she didn't believe it.

"Please Lord, share my pain," she prayed.

As she drifted off to sleep, a strange peace settled on her. Could it be the lulling sound of rain on the roof?

David's words after a damp camping experience echoed in her mind. "There's no better music to make you fall asleep than the drumming of rain on a roof."

She tugged the sheet up a little higher and listened closer.

"You were right, David," she whispered into the darkness as sleep claimed her, "Right about the rain ..."

Chapter 5

The alarm's shrill beep broke the early morning silence. Was it really six-thirty already? Half asleep, she reached out her arm and fumbled around, trying to find the clock. It wasn't where it ought to be. Hadn't it been right ...

She sat bolt upright, sleep forgotten. It hadn't been a dream. She was really here. The clock was on the table on the other side of the bed. She crawled out of the warm blankets to turn it off.

It was chilly in the house, and she shivered. Resisting the temptation to return to her snug nest, Jenny quickly pulled the sheets and blankets up, making the bed. She pulled on her jeans and a plain shirt, shivering as she dressed. She pulled her hair back into a short ponytail and rolled up the too-long hems on her jeans. She was ready for the day.

Jenny left her room, padded softly down the hall, and peeked in on Peter. He was still sound asleep, snuggled deeply into his warm bed. She smiled and continued down the hallway to the glass doors that opened onto the small balcony. She unlatched them, then gently pushed them open and stepped outside.

She breathed deeply of the morning. The rain-washed world was fresh and clean, and it had the most wonderful smell. Drops hung heavy on the balcony railing, and she put her finger underneath one, watching in fascination as the translucent bubble of water wavered between her skin and the iron rail. Dropping her finger, she watched as the drop stretched with it until, finally reaching the breaking point, it fell.

Steam rose off the pond, and fog drifted low in the valley near the eastern hills. On the lake hundreds of ducks paddled calmly, calling loudly to one another in the still air. The windmill in the corrals remained stationary, the blades of the fan shining in the rising sun's light. Had she stepped into a painting, or a fairy-land?

"When the morning shadows stretch across the land, before the early morning mists have flown, I'll show you all the land I know and proudly call ... my own."

Jenny shook her head, smiling. Where did all that come from? I haven't written poetry in years.

Yet the verse fit the day perfectly. Turning back into the house, she closed and locked the doors behind her. At the desk in her room, she rummaged around for a pencil and opened the notebook she had put there the night before. She wrote the short verse down. Then she closed the book and made her way downstairs to the kitchen.

She opened cupboard doors, looking for breakfast makings. Maybe muffins would be good. As she mixed them, she couldn't help but like the kitchen. It was large and had an island near the cupboards. The table and chairs fit neatly in the center of the room. Cupboards lined the east and south walls, and the refrigerator was near the door to the porch. The sink was centered under the large windows on the south wall and had a dishwasher next to it. The stove was on the west wall. The door to the pantry and the door into the dining room were on the north wall. Between the two doors was the telephone. There was also a built-in desk and her grandmother's sewing nook.

It was the nicest kitchen she'd ever seen, she decided. But it wasn't the polished oak cabinets or the big stove that she liked best. It was the homey touches, such as the worn spot of linoleum, the hand-embroidered wall hanging with a Bible verse, the hand-sewn curtains. They made it beautiful; they made it home. Filling the muffin tins, she slid the tray into the oven and set the timer.

"Mommy!" Jenny heard Peter call, and she hurried to see what was the matter. Coming to a halt at the foot of the stairs, she looked up and saw Peter sitting on the top stair, a shoe in one hand.

"Good morning, sweetie," she said. "What's wrong?"

"Mommy, I can't get this shoe on," he said in frustration, waving the shoe in the air.

The Bargain

"Well, come on down to the kitchen, and I'll help you."

Peter nodded and came downstairs. She lifted him onto a kitchen chair and took the shoe.

"Well, silly, it's the wrong foot." Jenny laughed, showing him. "See, this one goes on your right foot not your left."

Mike beat two eggs together and poured in a little milk. He'd overslept this morning, something he didn't do often.

Yesterday had been a strain, and he hadn't gotten to sleep until late last night. Even after he'd gotten to bed, his mind had kept working at a furious pace. There were times that he regretted making his dog sleep outside. He could have used someone to talk to last night, even if it did have four legs.

As he poured eggs in the skillet, Mike thought back to the young widow who was his new neighbor. How had she slept last night? And how was she going to manage that ranch all alone? Would she stay here, or would she sell the ranch and go back to Texas?

He recalled the look in Jenny's eyes as she stared at the valley. She would stay. He had the feeling that she had not had much in her life. The few boxes in the back of the old car, the little boy in clothes that were almost too small, the tired, haunted look in her eyes that seemed to thank him for even the smallest kindness ... it all added up. Or maybe he was just crazy.

He stirred the eggs and got a plate out of the cupboard.

The beautiful young widow reminded him of his own empty house. He was twenty-five years old and hadn't found a woman to share his life with yet. More than anything, he wanted a wife and family, but apparently God had other plans for the time being. He just kept praying. Someday, maybe ...

Curving his lips in a half-smile, he carried the eggs to the tiny table squeezed in the middle of the kitchen. There wouldn't be room for a woman in this house, even if he did find one. The tiny bedroom, bath, living room and kitchen were cramped for one. They certainly wouldn't hold two.

God's plans were perfect – hopefully they included a wonderful woman with a house. Mike laughed before bowing his head to bless the meager meal.

Finishing his prayer, he raised his head and opened the box of doughnuts he'd bought in town yesterday.

What did he have to do today? The windmills in the pastures needed to be checked, and he would have to put out more salt and mineral.

"I'd better check for my new neighbor too," he muttered. "Unless I miss my guess, she knows even less about ranching than I do about cooking. Maybe I should invite her and Peter to come along; they should start learning how a ranch works."

Jenny hung the last load of clothes on the line behind the house and carried the basket inside. Lunch was over, and she had convinced Peter to settle down for a short nap. Oh, what she wouldn't give for one as well.

Dropping the empty basket to the floor near the washer, she walked through the house to the living room. She pushed open the squeaky screen door, walked out onto the shadowed porch and sank down wearily in the swing. It would be good to sit here – just for a few moments.

She leaned her head back against the seat. It fit her just right. Letting her eyes drift shut, she listened to the birds chattering in the trees. She would just rest for a moment; then she would go work in the garden ...

Mike drove slowly into her yard and stopped near the salt shed. He'd finished checking his cattle, and now he was ready to help check Pete's – no, the widow's. Somehow it didn't seem as though Pete was really gone. He walked around the side of the pickup to the house.

Knocking gently on the back door, he received no answer. Well, he'd try the front door. She had to be home; her car was still parked out front.

As he rounded the tree that blocked the porch from

view, he saw her. She was sitting comfortably in the porch swing, head on her shoulder, eyes closed. Stepping softly onto the porch, Mike perched on the side wall, just watching her. She was wearing a big white shirt with the sleeves rolled up into cuffs and a pair of blue jeans. Her hair was pulled back, but small wisps surrounded her face. The heavy hiking boots on her feet were tiny compared to his huge, leather work boots. She was really a beautiful young woman. He leaned forward, speaking softly.

"Ma'am? Wake up, Ma'am."

Jenny slowly surfaced. There was someone talking to her, telling her to wake up. Was she asleep? It was too pleasant to be sleep – there were no dreams of David, no nightmares of screaming metal ...

"Ma'am?"

She opened her eyes, slowly focusing on the person in front of her. It was that man – Mike. He was sitting in front of her, leaning forward, elbows on his knees, hands holding a cap.

"Hi," she said, sitting up straighter. "Did I fall asleep?"

"Looks that way." he grinned. "But you picked a good place to do it."

"Sure did." Jenny tucked a stray strand of hair back.

The Bargain

"Ma'am, today's the day the cows need checked. I thought I'd go, but maybe you and Peter would want to come along and see how everything works."

"Yes." she nodded thoughtfully. "That would be nice. I'd better go wake Peter."

"Sure." Mike stood. "I'll go load the salt and mineral." He started across the lawn, then stopped and turned back. "I'll be over there, in the salt shed," he pointed.

"All right."

Jenny finished tying the laces on Peter's shoes and took his hand.

"Where we goin'?" Peter asked as she ushered him out the door.

"To see the cows," she explained.

"Yea! Cows!" Peter jumped up and down, pulled his hand from hers and raced across to where Mike's pickup was parked.

Jenny followed more slowly. Mike came out of the salt shed with two more sacks of something and swung them into the back of the pickup.

"Hey, Peter," he called as Peter ran up, "you going to help me check the windmills today?"

"Sure!" Peter answered. "What're windmills?"

Mike laughed, opening the driver's side door and letting Peter scramble inside.

"You've never seen a windmill? Well, my boy, today's your lucky day."

Jenny reached the pickup, and after a moment's hesitation, she opened the door and crawled in. She pulled the door shut as Mike started the engine. The inside of the truck was more ancient than the outside. The faded blue seat was torn in many places. Rope and tools were scattered on the floor beneath her feet. The dust-covered dash had a miniature calendar stuck to it, dated four years before. This was not the pickup Mike had been in yesterday. She said as much, and he grinned.

"Nope. This is a ranch pickup. It does all the work around here. The other one is what I drive to town, but around here, this is my third hand."

"Oh. Does ... did Grandpa have one?"

"Yep. It's parked in the shop. You two ready to go?"

"Yep!" Peter said, dodging as Mike stepped on the clutch and reached for the gear shift.

"Good." Mike started down the drive.

They passed the barn and the mailbox as they headed to the road they had taken yesterday. Jenny laid her arm on the window ledge.

"We're going to what we call the summer range," Mike said, glancing at Jenny and Peter. "That's where the cattle spend the summer. It's a great big pasture with some pretty big hills. The cows eat the grass all summer and raise their calves. Cattle need more than the grass, though. Four windmills and tanks provide water for them. It's the rancher's job to make sure that all the windmills are pumping water and the tanks hold the water. We also provide a salt and mineral supplement in feeders near the windmills. Those have to be replenished about once a week."

Jenny nodded. That would explain the sacks he'd loaded into the back. Mike pulled onto a short side road, and stopped before a barbed wire gate.

"I can get it," he said.

Jenny watched as Mike hopped out of the truck and hurried to the gate. He unlatched the lever from the gate and let it swing back, freeing the gate. Slipping the post from a bottom wire loop he pulled the gate open, the barbed wire strands dragging on the ground. He dropped it and trotted back to the truck. Hopping in, he drove through, not bothering to shut his door. He hopped back out again and shut the gate.

Jenny felt her face flush and hoped it didn't show. She should have opened the gate back there. If she had done it, it would have been much faster. She straightened her shoulders. Well, she would get the next one.

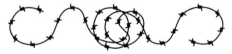

Mike grinned to himself as the emotions flitted across her face. Yep, she'd be getting the next gate. If she was as determined as he thought she might be, she just might be able to stick it out and make the ranch work. Only time would tell, though. There were a lot more gates to be opened, in more ways than one.

Chapter 6

The pasture road consisted of two uneven ruts winding among and over the hills. Jenny held her breath on more than one occasion, but not once did the pickup smash into the next hill. As they came into a particularly steep dip in the road, Mike kept up a running commentary, pointing everything out to Peter.

"See those funny marks in the road?" he asked. "They were made by birds."

Jenny wasn't sure how he saw them and managed to drive at the same time. Finally the pickup rounded a hill overlooking a valley, and they saw the first windmill. It was tall, a steel tower with a wheel on top. The wheel had angled blades, and it turned in the slight wind. A ladder was built onto the side of the tower. Jenny guessed this was for servicing the windmill. Water gushed from a horizontal pipe attached to a vertical pipe centered inside the tower's four legs. The water ran into a large tank, about twenty feet across. About another fifty yards from the tank was a strange contraption that looked like a hood sheltering a small rubber tub.

The Bargain

The tub contained a sandy-brown colored mixture.

Mike and Peter were standing by the tower before Jenny opened the door. She hopped out, her boots sinking in the sand.

"See, Peter, this is a windmill," Mike said, pointing upward. "Those blades called fans turn a motor. The motor is attached to a pipe that goes down inside the well to where the water is, and it makes the pipe lift the water up. The water then comes out the other pipe and fills the tank."

"Wow! It does all that?" Peter asked, following Mike as he walked over to the edge of the tank opposite the windmill.

Pointing to the small pipe sticking up out of the water by a bare half inch, Mike continued, "That's the overflow pipe. When the windmill pumps too much water to be held in the tank, the extra pours out through that and then into the pond over there." He pointed to a marshy-looking place ten yards from the windmill. Reaching over into the tank, he pulled a handful of dripping green algae off the overflow pipe. "You've got to keep it clean so the water doesn't over fill the tank."

Jenny nodded and then followed as Mike walked back to the truck. He pulled two sacks out, one partly used, the other new.

"Here, ma'am." He handed her the half-full sack. "You can carry this."

"Sure." She took it from him, her arms sagging downward with the weight. Mike swung the other sack easily to his shoulder and led the way to the strange contraption with the tub.

"This is the salt-feeder," Mike said. "The top part catches the wind and swings so that the tub inside is always protected from the weather."

"That's a good idea." Jenny agreed, readjusting her grip on the sack.

"Yep. I'm working on a new design, though. The cows can get their heads under this one and pull the top off. I've got an idea for one that might work better."

"You're building one?" Jenny asked incredulously.

"Sure." Mike grabbed a string and pulled it, easily opening his sack. He poured salt into the tub.

He set the sack on the ground and took the other sack from her. "This is mineral," he said, opening it and pouring red-brown crystals out.

"Peter, do you want to help me stir this together?" Mike asked, plunging his hand into the feeder to demonstrate.

"What's it for?" Peter asked.

"The cows lick it and get the minerals their bodies need."

"It's like sand, only bigger," Peter said, giggling as he plunged both small hands in to mix it.

"That's right," Mike said. "Do you want to stir, ma'am?"

"Sure!"

Jenny stuck her hand in. She grinned at Peter, drinking in the look of pure delight on his face.

"I can handle this." She smiled.

"Sure you can, ma'am," Mike said reassuringly.

"Please, call me Jenny," she said, standing up again. "If I call you Mike, the least you can do is return the favor." .

"All right."

"Besides." She smiled slightly. "I'll answer better to Jenny. Every time you say ma'am, I look around to see who you're talking to."

"Point taken, ma'a – Jenny," he doffed his cap, then let the breeze cool his head. "It's hot out, isn't it?"

"It's hot all right," Peter agreed, removing his hands from the mixture. He brushed them on his jeans before wiping the sweat from his forehead. "Mommy, I'm thirsty."

"You'll have to wait until we get home," Jenny said gently. She was thirsty too, although it was much cooler here than in Texas.

"Naw." Mike nodded toward the windmill. "We've got some of the best water in the world right here."

"You mean drink out of the tank?" Peter asked, his eyes wide.

"No, out of the pipe. You just bend over and drink out of it like you do out of a hose."

He glanced at their faces. "Well, maybe that's not the best way."

Moving to the pickup, Mike pulled the door open. Yanking open the glove box, he triumphantly held a sack of small paper cups aloft.

"Here you go! I bought these when my sister brought her kids out in June."

Mike walked back to the windmill, bent over the pipe and filled two cups with the sparkling cold water. He handed one cup to Peter and the other to Jenny.

She raised the cup to her lips and took a long drink. As she lowered the cup, she peered at the water, puzzled. It was pure and sweet tasting, cold, and very good.

"It's good!" She said in delight.

"Best water in the world," Mike assured her. "It comes from the Ogallala aquifer."

"And to think that I've been drinking the bottled water we brought north," she said almost to herself, "when I could have had this coming out of the tap."

"Mmm," Peter said, finishing his. "Thanks, Mike!"

"You're welcome, Peter." Mike grinned. "Now, we've got three more windmills to check."

He loaded the sacks into the back of the pickup and Jenny and Peter piled back into the truck, ready for whatever new adventure was before them.

Jenny glanced at her watch as she hopped back in the pickup after closing the last gate and was surprised to see that it was already four-thirty. They had spent three hours in the big pasture. Mike put the pickup in gear as she swung her door shut. They were back on the main road now, headed for home. She gazed out her window as they drove past the corner of the lake where it lapped the shore near the road. Soon they were beyond that, slowing as they neared the mailbox. Mike brought the truck to a stop and got out. He opened the mailbox and retrieved a twine-wrapped bundle before returning to the truck.

"Here," he handed it to Jenny as he closed his door and drove toward the house.

"Grandfather's mail," she said, glancing at the name on the outer magazine.

"Yeah, I forgot to get it yesterday."

"And the day before as well, by the looks of it." It was a fat bundle, more mail than she'd seen at one time.

"No, we just get mail on Monday, Wednesday and Friday."

"Doesn't it come six days a week?"

"No, this is a rural route, a really rural route." He glanced over at her. "Didn't you come to the country for a slower life?" he asked.

"All right, point taken." She smiled back. They were in the farmyard then, and he stopped the truck in front of the house.

She opened her door and got out, reaching to help Peter down, but he declined all assistance, leaping out on his own. She shut the door firmly and looked through the open window at Mike.

"Thanks for showing us everything. We had fun."

"You're welcome. I'll be back to ride herd on the cows on Thursday. If you don't mind horses, you're welcome to come along with me."

"Sure." She nodded, stepping back from the truck.

He backed out and was gone, leaving only a cloud of dust. Turning back to the house, she walked slowly across the yard.

Peter had disappeared from sight, but she heard him calling from the back yard.

"Kitty, come here kitty," he coaxed.

Inside, Jenny got a glass out of the cupboard and filled it with water from the tap. Savoring the sweetness, she gazed out the window at the family of Canada geese grazing in the meadow in front of the house. The air was filled with the calls of hundreds of birds, but it was a low sound, pleasant in the way that a mountain stream rushing over rocks is pleasant. She nearly jumped out of her skin when the phone rang. Crossing the kitchen, she grabbed it up before it rang again.

"Hello?"

"Hello, Mrs. Cook. Glad I finally caught you. Been calling all afternoon. This is Jon Carlisle, your granddad's attorney, remember?"

"Yes, Mr. Carlisle, I remember. How are you today?"

"Fine, thanks. Um ... We need to probate your grand-father's will. Can you make it to Ogallala by ten tomorrow morning? We'll get that done before lunch so you won't be driving home after dark."

"Ten? I think so."

"Good. Got a paper and pen?"

"Just a minute," she said as she reached for the small pad and pen on the table.

"OK."

She scribbled down the directions.

Leaning against the wall, she took a deep breath. The finality of everything was finally sinking in. Tomorrow the ranch became hers, for better or for worse. "God, help me make it work. Please help me," she prayed.

"Peter, bath time," Jenny called, drying her hands and turning the dishwasher on.

There was no answer.

"Peter," she called again.

Where was he? She hurried through the house but saw no sign of him. Where could he have gotten to?

"Peter!" She stepped out onto the front porch and breathed a sigh of relief. He was sound asleep on the porch swing, rocking slightly in the breeze.

His eyes opened, and he sat up. Reaching for his hand, Jenny helped him to his feet.

"You ready for your bath? We've got to get all that dirt off you before we go to town tomorrow."

Peter stopped, wrenching his hand free of hers. "No. Don't want a bath!" His lower lip stuck out stubbornly.

"Why not?"

"Like bein' dirty. If it gets washed off, it won't be fun anymore."

"You think that if all the dirt gets washed off, you won't get to be dirty again?"

He nodded, tears pooling in his eyes. "Don't wanna go to town. Don't wanna go home. It's awful there, and you're sad, an' I hate it!"

She knelt on the floor in front of him, and looked him in the eyes. "Honey, this is home." She smiled. "We're going to town tomorrow so Mommy can get the papers that say we can stay here."

"You sure?"

"Promise. Now, don't you want to be just a little bit clean?" She wrinkled her nose at him, grinning. "Or are you just going to stay dirty?" She tweaked his nose gently and picked him up. He giggled, his tears forgotten.

Mike put his magazine down and stared at the wall. All he could see was Jenny's face as she had been that afternoon. He could still see the stubborn line of her jaw as she wrestled the stiff gate open and the triumph when she finally opened it. She had learned how to pour the right amount of salt and mineral out and had asked questions about windmills until she knew as much about them as he did. She had fun doing it all; she hadn't been afraid to get dirty. In fact, she had encouraged her son to do so. Everything had been turned into a game, from counting cows to pulling apart grass.

Yet there had been an underlying reason for it all. There was still that indefinable sorrow in her eyes that didn't go away no matter how many times she laughed.

Peter had more fun than Mike had ever seen a little kid have, and he had it because his mom had been happy. For Peter's sake ... that was it. Everything she did was for that little boy, from laughing to living, just like everything her grandfather had done in the past few years had been for her.

As he rose from his chair and switched off the lamp, he still pictured her face, but it wasn't the laughing, joyful face of that afternoon. He saw deep, intense sorrow that had been there for a second, but so very real. He wished that he could take the pain away.

Preparing for bed, he recalled part of "Song of Songs."

" – for love is as strong as death, it's jealousy unyielding as the grave ..."

How would he feel if he had lost his wife? As though

the world was falling apart, he knew. In marriage, you were supposed to grow old together, not grieve forever.

"God," Mike prayed, "please give her back her life. Don't let her hurt forever."

With that he fell asleep, haunted by her sad brown eyes.

Chapter 7

"Sign here, ma'am, and that'll be it." Jon Carlisle pushed the pen and papers across the table to Jenny, and she signed her name neatly on the blank.

"Good. The accountant will send you the forms for the inheritance tax as soon as they're drawn up. Things are fixed up with the bank so your name is on the ranch checking account now. You can use the account any time, just remember to write everything down clearly so you can take your deductions. You getting all this, ma'am?" he asked.

Jenny smiled across the desk. "I think so. I just ... To be honest, I know nothing about ranches, Mr. Carlisle."

"You'll learn soon enough, I expect." He nodded knowingly.

"But until then ..." She shrugged with an honest smile. "I've just jumped into a very large ocean, and I have no idea how to swim."

"Keep your head above water, that's the important thing." Jon Carlisle smiled gently. "But if you need a life preserver now and then, ask Mike Snow. He's a good man, and he'll help you."

"He's already done so much."

"It doesn't matter to Mike; he helps everybody. Don't hesitate to ask if you need help." Jon Carlisle suddenly became very serious. "Ma'am, I know it's none of my business, but are you a Christian?"

"Yes." She smiled.

"Well so is Mike. He doesn't do things like most folks – for profit or for gain. The most payment he'll take is a prayer now and then."

"Thank you, Mr. Carlisle, for everything." Jenny tucked the checkbook into her purse before swinging it to her shoulder.

"Take care, ma'am." The lawyer stood up, as she moved to the door.

"You too." She nodded, pushing through the door into the hall.

Peter was in the small waiting area, sitting quietly until she entered the room. Then he jumped off the chair and ran to her, wrapping her in a big hug. She returned it, but realized again that he was clinging very close to her.

Ever since David died, things hadn't been the same. Peter was so afraid of losing her that he didn't let her out of his sight for more than an hour. She felt the same way about him.

"Ready for lunch?" Jenny asked, pushing her worries to the back of her mind.

"Yep. I'm hungry."

"Good. So am I," she declared.

As they stepped outside, Jenny dropped a hand to smooth the wrinkles from her skirt before climbing into the car. They had a quick lunch and bought some groceries before heading back to the ranch.

Three hours later, they were home. Jenny unloaded the groceries and after changing her clothes, worked in the garden for an hour picking beans. There were enough of the right size to can, and it was late before she finished. Jenny took a last peek under the towel on the table at the gleaming pints of beans. She and Peter would not go hungry this winter.

She fell into bed, and sleep came easily. Drifting off, she thought of the next day. She ought to do some baking ... and the house needed a little cleaning up. Oh, and Mike was coming to do something with the cows and horses.

Jenny gripped the reins tightly with her left hand and clung to the saddle horn with her right. The horse had not looked that big in the pasture, but now that she was on him, he was huge. She hadn't been on a horse since she was sixteen.

"How's it feel?" Mike asked.

She did a quick evaluation before answering.

"Good," she said. "If I weren't so far from the ground, I'd be set."

"Don't worry," Mike said. "Red is a complete gentleman." He smiled, and his dark eyes lit up reassuringly. "You'll do fine. All you need is practice."

He gathered his reins and mounted his horse in a single fluid motion, settling in behind Peter before turning the horse toward the corral gate that led into the meadow. Jenny nudged Red, and they followed at a trot. The saddle had a comforting creak as the leather moved with the horse.

I'm the boss; Red does what I tell him, she reminded herself, taking a deep breath and settling into the rhythm of the saddle. She relaxed as Red moved into a gallop at her urging, following Mike across the meadow toward the summer pasture gate.

The afternoon sky was a blue bowl; the cottony white clouds hung by invisible strings and were motionless. Peter's laugh drifted back to her, and she wondered again at the wisdom of allowing him to come. She couldn't leave him alone in the house, though, so there really wasn't much choice in the matter.

Mike rode the horse like it was a part of him. It probably was, she thought. Well she would learn. She might be scared to death right now, but eventually there would come a day when she would find it as easy as Mike did.

They approached the gate, and Mike dismounted and

opened it. He led his horse through, then let her follow before closing it. Swinging back into the saddle, he pulled his horse up beside hers.

"We're looking for any sick cattle, both cows and calves. If you see something that doesn't look right to you, let me know. Then we'll see what we can do about it. OK?"

She nodded, and they rode on. Peter chattered along happily. He was enjoying the ride, the day and life in general.

"What kind of cows are they, Mike? They don't look like the ones in my books," Peter said.

"They're black Angus," Mike answered.

"How do you milk 'em all?"

Mike burst into laughter. A few moments passed before he could speak again. "I'm sorry for laughing, Peter, but these aren't milk cows. I don't think you could get one gentle enough to milk it if you tried. They're beef cattle."

"Oh. They'd prob'ly give chocolate milk anyways."

Jenny felt herself about to laugh as Mike asked, "How do you figure that?"

"'Cause they're black. They got to be white to give white milk," Peter answered simply.

Jenny did laugh then. "Honey, I think all cows give white milk."

"Afraid so, Peter," Mike agreed with an impish twinkle in his eyes.

"Well, they ought to give chocolate milk. I'll bet the calves would like that better." Peter nodded knowingly.

How could she hurt so much? Jenny wondered as she walked to the house. They had found no sick cows or calves, much to her relief. They had ridden the whole pasture, though. When she had finally gotten off her horse, she had found her legs turned to jelly from the knees down. Her thighs were rubbed raw from where she had sat in the saddle, and her arms ached. Every muscle and bone felt sore from Red's bone-jarring trot. Even the smooth gallop had taken more energy than she had.

Peter scampered along beside her as they reached the yard, seemingly unaffected from the long ride.

"Can I have a cookie, Mommy? I'm awful hungry, just like Red. Did you see him eat? He's so funny! And the cows are even funnier. They chew like ..." He paused, giving her a demonstration. "Boy, I couldn't eat grass."

"I couldn't either," she said with a smile as she opened the screen door. "Why don't we have that cookie with ice cream?"

"Mmm!" Peter grabbed a kitchen chair and was starting to climb for bowls when she lifted him to the floor.

"There'll be no ice cream until you wash your hands;

they smell like horse."

"All right." Peter galloped through the house to the bathroom. Jenny leaned against the kitchen sink and began washing her own hands.

She quickly prepared the snack then left Peter to his own devices. She dropped her tennis shoes on the porch floor and padded upstairs. She found a cool summer dress while hot water ran in the big tub. Then she sank into the tub with a weary sigh and leaned her head back, closing her eyes as the hot water eased her aching muscles.

How was she going to make a rancher? It hurt too much. A despair she hadn't felt before welled up inside. She had to ride the pasture twice a week. Was it always going to be like this? What happened if a cow or calf actually got sick? Could she take care of it? What if ...

No. She told herself forcefully. She couldn't look at the worst side of things and remain sane. She had done a good job today. She had stayed on the horse; she had ridden the whole pasture; and she was still alive. The cattle were fine, and Peter had fun. That was enough for now. Sinking deeper into the water, she said a prayer of thanks.

Jenny found her way to bed early. Peter was tired after missing his nap, and she was exhausted. Easing between the cool sheets, she flicked off the bedside lamp. Closing her eyes, she discovered that, as tired as she was, sleep would not claim her. She kept remembering the wind in her face and the horse's hooves pounding the ground. Picturing Mike's beautiful gray horse, she saw Peter laughing in front of him. But no ... it wasn't Mike she saw riding ... it was David.

"Oh, David ..."

The next thing Jenny knew, the alarm was ringing, and it was morning. As she rolled over to turn the clamoring off, yesterday returned in a flash of pain. It was all she could do to make it to the bathtub again. An hour later, she almost felt like starting the day. She poured bowls of cold cereal, made toast for breakfast and greeted Peter cheerfully when he came downstairs. Dressed in jeans and a long-sleeve shirt, he galloped in on an old stick horse he'd found on the back porch.

"Mornin', cowboy." Jenny smiled. "Park your horse, and I'll serve breakfast."

"Yes'm."

He doffed an imaginary hat and propped the horse up next to the table before climbing onto a chair.

"Wa'al puncher, what're ya gonna do today?" She stretched out her drawl and poured juice.

"I'm gonna go check all the cows, and then I'm gonna doctor the sick ones like Mike."

"That's a pretty big job," Jenny said.

"Can I ride Red today, Mommy?"

"I don't think Mommy would like that," she groaned.

"Mike promised to teach me how to hold the reins," Peter said proudly.

"That's good. Why don't you eat breakfast, then we'll see what we have to do today."

"OK," he agreed, picking up his spoon.

Jenny pulled out her chair and sat gingerly, silently vowing to never get on a horse again if she could help it.

On Sunday morning, Jenny found herself in front of the small church Mike had invited her to. Peter was white-faced beside her; he had been carsick again. She nervously smoothed her dress and started toward the door. They were early, but other people were trickling into the building. Stepping inside, she blinked in the dimness and saw a young woman coming toward her.

"Hello," the woman greeted them and reached out to shake hands. Blond hair framed her face with its sparkling, gray eyes. "I'm Laurie Richards."

"I'm Jenny Cook, and this is Peter," Jenny said, as the two women shook hands.

"Well, Jenny Cook, I'm glad you could come. We don't have a large congregation, so we welcome all recruits." Laurie grinned mischievously.

A tall man hurried from the pews beyond to Laurie.

"Honey, where did you leave your guitar?"

"In the pickup," Laurie said, grabbing his hand as he turned to leave. "Frank, meet Jenny and Peter Cook."

"Hi," Frank said as he turned his attention to his wife. He turned back and said, "Sorry I'm so abrupt. We don't want to scare anyone off."

"Don't worry," Jenny said, "I don't scare easily."

"Good. Laurie, Mrs. Trippe is sick. Pastor wonders if you can handle the music."

"Oh no. We had everything worked out."

"Pray about it," Frank suggested. "I'll go get the guitar."

"What's wrong?" Jenny asked, as Frank hurried outside.

"I need someone to play the piano while I get the kids organized. Today's the annual Grandparent's Day pageant, and the kids need all the help they can get. The problem is that no one plays the piano except for Mrs. Trippe, and now she's sick."

"Mommy plays the piano real good," Peter piped up.

"I haven't practiced in ..."

"You play though?" Laurie asked quickly.

"Sort of, but ..."

"Good. As of now, you're drafted." Laurie wrapped an arm around Jenny's shoulder and pulled her into the sanctuary. "We've got just enough time to show you the ropes before the service starts."

"What about Peter?"

"I've got three boys who would love to meet him," Laurie assured her.

They stopped at a pew, and Laurie gave three young boys stern instructions concerning their visitor. Then she pulled Jenny toward the piano. Jenny had just enough time to smile reassuringly at Peter before she found herself in front of a keyboard and a hymnal.

Mike hurried into church a few moments before the service started. He scanned the congregation for Jenny, but he didn't see her. Disappointed, he slipped into the pew next to Frank and his angelic ruffians.

"Hey, Frank," he greeted him.

"Hi, Mike. How's life? We missed you last week."

"Peter Riley died, and I was getting everything ready for his granddaughter to come." Mike sat down and reached for a hymnal.

"I hadn't heard. I'm sorry, Mike. I know how much he meant to you."

"Thanks, Frank. How are Laurie and the kids?"

"Laurie's busy getting everything ready for the program. The kids are fine. They've got a new friend today."

"Oh?"

"Yeah. Laurie recruited his mom to play the piano, so he's sitting with us. He's a cute little guy."

The Bargain

Mike peered around Frank at the row of little boys, between the ages of three and six. They were blonds with blue eyes, but there was one exception, and Mike stared.

"Hi, Mike!" Peter Cook grinned. "Is this your church too?"

Mike didn't have time to say anything. Music spilled forth from the piano, and he joined everyone else as they stood. His breath caught in his throat. There behind the piano sat Jenny Cook, dark hair upswept and eyes shining. Mike felt his heart skip a beat.

Chapter 8

"Thank you for helping me out," Laurie said again as Jenny slid into the car.

Closing the door, Jenny looked through the open window. "I enjoyed it, very much."

"Good. You'll have to come have dinner with us after church next week."

"We'll try," Jenny promised.

"All right." Laurie stepped away reluctantly. "I'll call you sometime this week."

"I'd love that."

Jenny watched Laurie walk slowly away, feeling as though she had just found a wonderful new friend.

Jenny started the car and pulled away from the curb. She glanced over at Peter. He was buckled in, eyes shut as he leaned back against the seat.

"Are you ready to go home, honey?"

"Yeah, Mommy. I just wish that road liked me better."

Lost in her own thoughts, Jenny didn't hear him.

"Hmm?" She asked, turning onto the highway.

The Bargain

"Maybe I wouldn't get so sick then."

"I'm sorry, Peter. I know it hurts. How about if we stop half way home so you can walk around a little. OK?"

"OK."

The next few weeks flew by. September gave way to October, and Jenny fell into a rancher's routine. Her friendship with Laurie grew through phone calls, weekly visits at church and at dinner afterward. Peter loved playing with Jimmy, Jon and Joel while their mothers talked. Mike was often there too, enjoying Frank's company.

On the ranch, Jenny and Peter put out salt and mineral and checked the windmills. Mike still helped ride the big pasture, and Jenny went from being sick with pain after riding to enjoying it, as they checked the cattle. Her skills on horseback progressed as well.

Peter helped her harvest the garden, enjoying digging the potatoes most of all. Soon, orange pumpkin and white and yellow squash joined the many gleaming jars of canned vegetables in the root cellar behind the house.

Mike brought his big tractor and special hay sled and moved the huge haystacks from the meadow into the fenced stack yards to form long, golden rows. When he refused payment, Jenny invited him to dinner. She questioned him about everything, learning all she could. Peter loved to have Mike there, and he developed a close friendship with him.

Nights grew chilly, and one morning, Jenny was surprised to see a glistening white frost covering the land. The idyllic days passed quickly. The mornings were always cool, sometimes almost bitter, but Jenny slipped into believing that autumn would last forever. That was not to be.

On the next to last Sunday in October, Jenny awoke snuggled deep under two heavy comforters and an afghan. She stretched and gazed out the window where great white flakes drifted lazily from the overcast sky. The honking of geese flying overhead was another reminder that fall seemed to be over. Jenny stared at the changed world outside the window.

Peter came padding into her room a few minutes later. He was dragging his stuffed rabbit by one ear. Sliding into Jenny's warm nest, he grinned and pointed to the window.

"Snow, Mommy. And it's not even Christmas!" Pure delight filled his face, and she couldn't help smiling back.

"Yes. Isn't it pretty?"

"Yeah."

The Bargain

Together they watched the wonder of it. Peter had seen snow only once before.

"Mommy?"

"Hmm?"

"What do the cows eat when the grass is under snow?"

The same question had come to her just moments before, and she was ready with an answer.

"I think they eat the haystacks."

"How? The cows are in the pasture, and the stacks are in the stack yards."

"Well ... I think the haystacks are taken to the cows on a sled like Mike's."

"Will we do that?"

"I don't know." She shrugged. "You sure have a lot of questions for this early in the morning. Why don't you go get dressed, and I'll cook us some breakfast?"

"OK."

Peter bounded out of the bed and took off down the hall to his room.

Jenny sat up, staring at the snow. How would she feed the cows? What did she have to do? It had been so easy up to now just checking on them. Why did it all have to change?

Everything changes, she reminded herself. Everything happens according to God's plan.

Jenny swung her feet out of bed and began dressing. She would not attempt the roads to church today. The tires on her car were almost bald. Maybe I'll invite Mike to Sunday dinner and ask a few questions, she thought.

She started breakfast, then called Mike.

"Hi!" she said when he answered.

"Jenny?"

"Yes. I see autumn suddenly became winter this morning."

"Sure did. I'll bet Peter likes it," Mike said.

"Yes, he does. I don't think we'll make it to church this morning in the snow. I wondered, if you don't have other plans, if you would like to come have Sunday dinner with us?"

"Yes!" He was enthusiastic.

"Like my cooking that much?" she asked.

"If you had to live on my cooking ..."

"That bad?"

"Let's just say I'll be coming to dinner with an appetite."

"Good. At twelve, then?"

"Sure, I'll be there."

"All right," she laughed. "Goodbye."

"'Bye."

Jenny hung up the phone and rescued the pancakes. Peter was waiting at the table, drinking his juice.

"Here you go, kiddo." She flipped a pancake shaped like a rabbit onto his plate and helped him get the syrup. After she fixed her own plate, Jenny turned the stove off and began planning the noon meal and the questions she wanted to ask Mike.

He's going to earn this dinner, she laughed to herself.

"Cake? I have to feed my cows cake?" Jenny was incredulous.

Mike couldn't help laughing at her expression as he passed her the roast beef.

"Cake," he said, "is a type of pressed, ground cottonseed for the cattle."

"Oh." She looked relieved, forked a piece of meat onto her plate and helped Peter fill his. Dinner smelled delicious.

"Actually," Mike said, "you don't have to worry about feeding for another week or two. First you have to get through sale day."

"Sale day?" she asked.

"Sale day means selling your calves. It happens next week. I would have told you earlier, but I thought I should wait until I checked the prices."

"Selling the calves ... that's what brings in the ranch income, right?"

"Yeah. Everything depends on the price you get for those calves out there."

"How are they sold?"

"Through the sale barn." Mike took a drink of iced tea. "On Friday, or maybe Saturday, if the weather's good," he continued, " we'll bring the herd into the corrals and sort the cows from the calves. Then we'll sort the calves. You need to keep some heifers to replace the old cows and maybe a steer to butcher, but you sell the rest. Trucks will come and take them to Ogallala to the sale barn. The sale's on Saturday. I'm selling too, so if you'd like, you and Peter can come with me. The sale barn is a whole different world, and unless you're used to it, it can be confusing."

"I've no doubt of that."

"After the calves are sold, you'll get a check. You put that in the bank, and that's your operating money for the next year."

"You make it sound simple."

"It is, in a way."

Jenny remembered those words Friday as Red pranced beneath her in front of Mike's barn. They were gathering Mike's cattle today. Hers would be brought in tomorrow, the day of the sale. It had been a busy week. Both her cattle and Mike's had been moved from the big summer pasture into ones closer to their barns.

Frank led his horse from the trailer, stripped off the halter and replaced it with a bridle. Laurie had brought the boys and insisted on watching Peter and cooking dinner.

The Bargain

"Let's move it," Mike called to Frank and Jenny. He was wide-eyed and ready to go at six in the morning.

"Just waitin' on you, slow poke," Frank returned good-naturedly.

Jenny smiled and nudged Red gently, starting him toward the gate. She had the hood on her grandfather's old down-filled coat pulled snugly. The morning was chilly, but the snow from Sunday had melted, and the day promised to be a good one.

"C'mon, Red, move!" Jenny shouted. Her hood flapped back and her hair blew in the wind as Red ran. A cow was leaving the herd and running straight between Red and the fence. As the cow loomed larger, Red wheeled and cut her off, loping alongside until she rejoined the herd. Jenny said a silent prayer of thanks and glanced over at Frank. He was roving back and forth behind the herd, urging it on.

Mike suddenly appeared, loping over a hill, his horse flying behind a cow and calf. They joined the herd, and as Mike circled the cattle, he gave Jenny the thumbs-up signal and a cheerful grin. The cattle moved on toward the corral, bawling loudly. Jenny held Red to a walk and felt a smile stretch across her face. She felt more alive this morning than she had in a long time.

Cattle milled around in the corral, dodging the men

as Mike and Frank moved through them. Jenny took a better hold on the heavy, iron gate and waited for the signal to open it. Red and the other two horses were cropping grass near the fence, their reins trailing. Soon a steady stream of cows moved past her through the gate, leaving the calves in the corral. Then Jenny chained the gate shut and crawled onto the fence. Mike and Frank began sorting the calves, and she watched with interest.

Frank opened and shut another gate as Mike chased the calves toward him. When Mike hollered, "Keep," Frank pulled the gate open and let the calf through. When Mike yelled, "Let 'em go," Frank did just that. After the calves were sorted, Mike and Frank sorted again, culling the scrubby-looking heifers.

An hour later, Jenny gathered the reins of Mike's horse and led him to the barn. Two huge cattle trucks were loaded with bawling calves. Frank and Mike checked the loads while Jenny unsaddled Mike's horse, turning him into the now deserted lot. Jenny caught up with Mike as he rounded the second truck and waved it on.

"I'm going to follow the trucks to town to make sure everything goes all right," Mike said to Jenny as he hurried toward the house. "I'll be back in time to do chores, and we'll round up your calves in the morning."

"All right." Jenny nodded.

Jenny watched the cattle trucks go, then joined Frank

next to his pickup. He was loading Red in the trailer.

"Hop in," Frank offered, shutting the trailer door.

Jenny climbed in, Frank following suit a few moments later. He turned the key, and the pickup roared to life.

When they arrived at Jenny's ranch, Frank let her out in front of the barn and helped her unload Red. She unsaddled the horse while Frank parked in front of the house.

Jenny liked the tall cowboy. He was the opposite of his wife, Laurie, and yet they were much the same. While Laurie was quick to speak and act, Frank thought things out. Both were wonderful people.

She turned Red out and headed for the house, shedding her filthy tennis shoes outside the back porch. After hanging her coat on the rack, she washed in the porch sink and went into the house.

"Mmm, what smells so good in here?" Jenny asked with a smile, sniffing the air. Laurie was mashing potatoes, keeping an eye on the bubbling gravy on the stove. The boys were in a row in front of the kitchen sink, splashing water every which way as they washed for dinner.

"Hi, Mommy!" Peter turned from the sink. "Guess what I did this morning? Joel an' me built a huge city down the hall upstairs. Then we played a game with Jon and Jimmy, an' after that ..."

"Slow down, fella." Jenny smiled. "Don't you have a

hug for your Mom?"

"Sure!" He wrapped his arms around her neck, then he broke free and ran after Joel into the dining room.

"Hey! No running in the house," Laurie called after them.

"Sorry!" The call drifted back.

"How'd it go?" Laurie asked, turning back to Jenny and Frank.

"Great," Frank said. "Miss Jenny is good help."

"I didn't fall off the horse, anyway," Jenny agreed. "Mike's on his way to town behind the trucks, and I know enough that I'll do much better tomorrow."

"Good," Laurie said as she carried two steaming bowls into the dining room. "Because you'll be working in the dark."

"Pardon?"

Laurie poked her head back through the doorway, eyes sparkling. "Tomorrow's the day of the sale. To get the trucks to the sale barn in time, you have to round up early."

"How early?"

"Four or four-thirty."

"A.M.?"

Chapter 9

The kitchen light reflected off the dark windows as Jenny mixed juice and poured herself a glass. Dressed in jeans and a warm flannel shirt, she was wide awake. The hands of her watch seemed perfectly normal, it was just the time that was not. When had she last been awake at four o'clock in the morning? Certainly not since Peter had been a baby.

Headlights arced through the darkness into the kitchen as a vehicle pulled up near the back door. Gulping down the last swallow of juice, Jenny set the glass in the sink and hurried to flick on the porch light. Opening the door to the chill morning air, she stepped aside as Laurie entered, her youngest son asleep in her arms. Frank followed, one son on his shoulder and the other stumbling beside him.

"Thank you so much for coming," Jenny whispered.

"What are friends for?" Laurie said. "These fellas will sleep another hour or two. Do you have somewhere they can lie down?"

"Sure." Jenny led the way upstairs to her room.

The Bargain

Back downstairs, Laurie took off her coat as Jenny put hers on.

"I'll get Peter up in time to go," Laurie assured her. "And I'll find something to cook for breakfast. I'll be praying for all of you."

Jenny turned from the door and hugged her. "Thank you, Laurie."

Laurie smiled. "You'd better go, or they'll have the whole herd rounded up without you."

Jenny slipped outside into the cold, dark morning. Overhead, the stars were slowly fading away. The light above the barn was on, casting a yellow pool over the corral. Frank had his horse there and was checking the cinch. As she stumbled to the barn, Jenny silently thanked God for giving her such wonderful friends.

"Morning," Mike greeted her as she entered the barn. "You look wide-awake."

"Good morning. I guess I'm just excited."

"Yeah? I am too, a little. You ever tried to round up black Angus in the dark? That's exciting."

Jenny laughed and reached over and stroked Red's neck. Mike fastened the back cinch and untied Red's reins, handing them to her. As she led the horse outside, she saw Frank was already mounted, his horse dancing below him.

"I hope Red's got better night vision than I do. Otherwise it's going to be a really short ride," Jenny said.

"The sun will be up soon," Frank assured her. Jenny glanced to the east and saw that he was right. A faint lightness was pushing back the dark sky as Mike flicked off the barn light. When her eyes adjusted, Jenny saw the dark shadow of the windmill looming high above them and the corrals around them. She nudged Red in the ribs, and they started out the east corral gate into the pasture.

Dawn came and went, the sun rising high and burning away the bitter cold of night. The day was fair, promising warmth as Jenny and Red worked. At 6:30, Mike sorted the last heifer calf through the gate and closed it. The cows were in the pasture, and Frank and Jenny were loading the trucks. Soon even that was done, and Frank gathered the horses' reins as Mike and Jenny checked the calves in the trucks. Then Mike waved the trucks on, and they hurried to the house.

Inside, they each had just enough time to grab a cinnamon roll before Peter came in, dressed and ready to go. Laurie's boys were close behind. Jenny and Mike finished eating at the same time, but they both declined seconds. Frank had no such inhibitions. He sat up to the table and accepted breakfast on a grand scale – rolls, scrambled eggs, hot oatmeal and bacon.

"If you're ready, we'll go," Mike said, as Jenny washed her hands. He had already pulled on his coat and was helping Peter into his. Jenny nodded and hurried to the bathroom, exchanging her shoes for hiking boots along the way. Then she grabbed her purse and a warm coat and hurried outside.

Peter was waiting in Mike's pickup, and when she climbed in, she had just enough time to shut her door before Mike had the truck in gear. They flew down the gravel road, headed to the sale.

It was after nine o'clock when Mike pulled into the parking lot in front of the sale barn. A line of trucks waiting to unload cattle stretched across the south half of the parking area. It almost blocked the entrance from the street. Jenny was looking at everything, and Mike wondered what she was thinking.

"Mommy, I have to go to the bathroom," Peter said.

Jenny glanced at Mike, and he smiled in what he hoped was a reassuring manner.

"Don't worry," he said. "It will be awhile before the trucks unload, so why don't we go in now."

She nodded and opened her door, helping Peter out. Mike got out and reached for his coat buttons. The day had warmed enough that his denim and sheepskin jacket was too warm. Tossing his coat onto the seat, he saw Jenny do the same with hers and Peter's.

They started for the door of the building that proclaimed itself to be the "Livestock Auction Market" of Ogallala.

"The most important day of a rancher's life, and I show up dressed like this," Jenny murmured, mostly to herself. Mike glanced over at her. A soft, red flannel shirt was tucked into her jeans, flattering her slim figure. Her dark hair was braided down the back, simple, yet very pretty. Her heart-shaped face was tanned from the summer sun, setting off her large, dark-brown eyes. She was a beautiful woman.

"You're dressed exactly like everyone else will be," Mike assured her. "You'll fit right in."

"I hope so."

"You look fine."

He held the glass door for her and Peter to enter, then stepped in behind them. Peter and Jenny both stopped, taking in the lobby with wide eyes. Mike looked around and saw again what they were seeing for the first time.

Weathered gray boards lined the walls. Facing them, a steep staircase led up, into the auction ring. The air was clean, but by night it would be full of smoke from the countless cigarettes smoked by the men who inhabited the orange plastic couches.

A pair of steer horns hung over the restroom doors in one corner. The wall to the left had a glass door and window looking into the restaurant. Paintings of the old west hung on the walls.

Opposite the restaurant, a long, high desk with a sign above it served the brand inspector. The center of activity, however, was the desk on the right side of the stairway. The words "Sellers" and "Buyers" were branded on the wall above the desk. Piles of papers and small pink cards littered the counter. Behind it, several women sat at their desks, busy with computers as they began the day's work.

Mike knew and loved the sights and sounds of the sale barn, but he was suddenly anxious that Jenny might not like them at all.

As she turned to face him, a smile stretched across her face.

"Is it always like this?" Jenny asked excitedly.

"On sale day, yes, and it gets much busier."

"Mommy!" Peter tugged on her hand.

"I know, I know." She started toward the restrooms, but Mike took Peter's hand.

"I'd better take him from here."

"All right. Thank you."

Mike found Jenny waiting near the door when he and Peter came out. They went outside, and he gave the information on Jenny's calves to the men unloading the trucks. Returning, Mike got two lists from the buyers desk and handed one to Jenny.

"What is this?"

"It's a list of all the cattle that will be sold today," Mike said, flipping through the pages. Finally he found what he was looking for.

"Here, look at this." He handed the sheet to her, and she glanced at it, unsure of what she was looking at.

"That's my name on there!" she said, surprised. "Jenny Cook, Bar R Angus," she read aloud.

"Top billing." Mike grinned.

"You're here too," she commented, flipping pages.

"Yep. Why don't we go get seats? If we wait much longer, the place will be full."

Jenny nodded.

Mike led the way up the steep staircase, through the swinging doors at the top and into the auction arena. Jenny and Peter were right behind him. He saw three empty seats halfway down the right side.

Leading the way through the smoky, dust-filled atmosphere, he shuffled between seat backs and knees with Jenny close behind until they reached their seats. Pulling the seats down, he helped Peter sit before he took a seat too.

"Hey, Mike!" a voice beside him said. Looking over, he saw the man who bought his calves year after year.

"Hello, Ben. How're prices?"

"Good for you, but not for me." The older man shifted position, oblivious to the din from the ring in front of them. "Who's your lady friend?"

"That's Jenny Cook, Pete Riley's granddaughter."

"Oh yeah? The buyers know who she is?"

"Not yet. I haven't seen Wagner yet. He usually buys Pete's calves."

"If I see him, I'll tell him," Ben promised, glancing back at his list.

The Bargain

The auctioneer shouted, "Sold! For ninety-eight and a quarter. That's all for the J Bar. Thank you, Paul and Mark Jorgenson.

"All right folks, we're moving on to the Diamond 3 Cattle Company. Turn to page six."

A gate clanged open, and a bawling, dusty herd of calves entered the ring, churning in a circle of red and white. One of the men in the ring squeezed the gate shut behind them. A head count appeared on the electronic board, along with the average weight of each animal and the group weight. The pen that held the calves was also a scale.

"Look at these pretty, little red heifers folks. They've had all their shots and are as green as those hills out yonder. These little ladies are fresh off the grass, just like they raise 'em out at the Diamond."

Mike glanced over at Jenny as the auctioneer started the bidding. She had flipped to page six and was listening closely to the rhythmic chant from the loudspeakers. Peter was watching with rapt attention as well, and Mike grinned. Kids didn't make a lot of noise in the sale barn for the simple reason that they were drowned out.

Three hours later, Jenny was quickly scribbling the average weight of a group of calves down next to their quantity in her book. As the price went up, she looked the calves over, learning what the buyers were looking for. Almost as fast as the calves were herded into the ring, they were taken out again through another gate. Another group was brought in, and the bidding continued. The auctioneer was selling truckloads of calves; an entire truckload could not fit into the ring at the same time. When the price was announced, she quickly wrote it down.

On the ride into town, Mike had told Jenny what to expect, and now she was beginning to understand what he had been talking about. The calves were sold by their weight. If a group of calves brought 98.25, that meant the seller was getting that many cents for every pound of every calf sold in that bunch. She had begun noticing that if the calves were black – Angus or another breed – they brought even more money. If each calf in a group weighed between 450 and 500 pounds, they brought the best price.

Her thoughts were interrupted as Mike leaned over and shook her sleeve.

"Are you ready to go eat?" he asked.

"Sure." She nodded, in case he didn't hear her.

"Come on then."

She rose from her seat and followed Mike and Peter down the row. Glancing at her watch, she saw it was almost one o'clock.

They made their way down the stairs to the lobby and were headed to the restaurant when Mike spotted someone and suddenly changed course. As she and Peter followed, they approached an old man wearing jeans and boots. He had a pink buyers card in his shirt pocket. The heavy black numbers declared him to be number 124.

"Mr. Wagner?" Mike asked.

"Yes?"

"I'm Mike Snow. I believe we met last year when Peter Riley and I joined you for lunch."

"Ah! Now I remember. Where is Pete? I haven't seen him yet, and I ..."

"Pete died a couple of months ago."

"I'm sorry to hear that. Who's running his place?"

"Mr. Wagner, I'd like you to meet Pete Riley's granddaughter, Jenny Cook. She'll be running the ranch now."

"Good day, Miss Cook." He turned his attention to Jenny and shook her hand. "I'm sorry about your grandfather. I saw your calves – in fact, I have my eye on them. They're a good-looking bunch."

"Thank you." She noticed Peter was hanging back. Reaching behind her, she pulled him gently forward. "This is Peter, my son."

"Why, hello, Peter." The old gentleman bent down and shook Peter's hand. "Would you like to join me for dinner?"

Peter nodded shyly, and Mr. Wagner smiled delightedly.

"Good! I hate to eat alone." He led them through the door into the restaurant.

When they were finished eating, Jenny took Peter to wash his hands. Charlie Wagner looked across the table at Mike and suddenly became very serious.

"Mike, I know this is none of my business, but I'm an old man, and if nothing else let me have my say."

"Go ahead."

"Don't let that young lady get away from you, Mike. She's something special – one in a million. I know she's grieving now, but I know grief, and it won't last forever. When I lost my Ellie ..."

He glanced up and saw Jenny and Peter returning. "Don't let her get away. She'll make a wonderful wife."

As Jenny made her way back to the table, Mike nodded thoughtfully and said, so quietly that Charlie barely heard him, "I know."

Chapter 10

Jenny shifted position as the latest bunch of calves escaped the sale ring. Peter had fallen asleep beside her. He was curled up in the seat. On her other side, Mike sat jotting down prices. His long limbs should have felt awful after spending hours in the chair, but he looked relaxed and alert. With the exception of a few trips to the lobby or to the corrals outside to see which pen their calves were in, they had spent all afternoon at the auction arena. She glanced at her watch. It was after four, and still their calves had not been sold. Her muscles were stiff from sitting.

Mike had offered to take her shopping, but she had been afraid she would miss seeing the calves sell. How much longer? The question plagued her, and she leaned over and whispered it to Mike.

"I don't know, but I'll tell you this: The price just went up about four cents a pound. Anytime in the next hour or so, and we'll get the best prices of the day."

His optimism put to rest her fears that they might not sell at all, and she settled back to watch the sale. Her eyes drifted away from the ring, and she observed the people in attendance. They were as diverse as the cattle that passed through the ring.

There were old farmers in bib overalls and seed company caps sitting near the stairs. Across the ring was a young man in jeans and a Western shirt talking on a cellular phone – an order buyer, Mike had explained earlier. No doubt he was talking to the men he bought cattle for.

A pretty woman dressed much like Jenny was writing prices on her sheet while entertaining a little girl with blond pigtails. A family of five with grandma and grandpa sitting next to them took up one whole row down by the sale ring. A teen-age boy in a sloppy sweatshirt and rundown tennis shoes sat next to one of the best-dressed ranchers in the room – father and son. Another father sat on the wooden steps and gently rocked a baby carrier, a diaper bag near his feet.

There was a lapse in the auctioneer's singsong sales pitch, and Jenny looked to see what was going on. The auctioneer was switching seats with the man next to him. Removing the microphone from its holder, the new auctioneer raised it to his lips and glanced at the paper in his hand.

"All right folks, we're moving on to Mike Snow's cattle. We'll be looking at a hundred and eighty head of pure Angus, starting with thirty head of heifers. Mike, where are you?"

The auctioneer searched the crowd, and Mike raised his hand.

"Good to see you, Mike. Now, these little ladies have had all their shots, including Bangs vaccinations. They're good, green as the grass on them hills. Folks, you know you can't pass up a money-making deal like this."

The auctioneer began the bidding, and Jenny felt Mike tense beside her. This was the cumulation of every day spent with the cattle all year long.

In the end, Mike received better than a dollar a pound for his best steers and heifers and just a little more for the smaller animals. Jenny spontaneously reached over and squeezed his hand.

"Good job," she congratulated him, a smile stretching across her face.

"I –"

Whatever he was about to say was cut off as another herd of black Angus calves ran into the ring.

"These are the Bar R Angus," the auctioneer began. "Folks, we're missing one of our number today. Pete Riley left us a couple of months ago. Today, we'd like to welcome his granddaughter, Miss Jenny Cook. Jenny, will you please stand?"

Mike squeezed her hand, and she stood up, feeling the eyes of everyone on her. She was tired, dirty and wrinkled after the long day. But to the crowd, she was one of them – a young person being handed the reins of the family ranch in a time-honored tradition.

Jenny sat down, and the auctioneer began. She moved to the edge of her seat. Her calves brought about the same as Mike's had. As the last bunch moved from the ring, she sat back and figured a total. Her mouth dropped open at the sum.

An hour later, Mike signaled for her to stand and leave. Then, reaching for Peter, he lifted the small boy and carried him to the lobby, following Jenny down the steep steps. Reaching the bottom, Mike gently guided Jenny to the sellers desk and asked for their checks.

The woman behind the desk smiled. "It'll be about thirty more minutes. Why don't you folks go have supper?"

"Thanks."

Jenny began coughing in the blue haze that filled the lobby. Mike took her elbow with his right hand and steered her to the door. Stepping out into the brisk night air, she took a deep breath before following Mike across the parking lot. The lights of the trucks waiting to load up defined their forms in the dark. Lights from the barn and the maze of pens drifted over the parking lot, pushing back the darkness.

Reaching the truck, Mike opened her door and slid Peter gently inside. Jenny eased in next to Peter and shut her door quietly. Mike got in and started the pickup, turning on the heater.

"Well, Jenny, where do you want to go for supper?"

"You choose. You know the town much better than I do."

"All right. You'd better wake Peter up, though." He put the pickup in gear, and Jenny leaned over and fastened Peter's seat belt before gently shaking him.

"Peter, honey, time to wake up."

A few minutes passed before Peter sat up, yawning sleepily. "Where are we?"

"We're in Ogallala, going to supper," Jenny said as she smoothed his rumpled hair. "Are you hungry?"

"Yeah."

"Good," Mike replied, "because here we are."

As they waited to be seated, Jenny looked with interest at the furnishings. Old wood-burning stoves, saddles, horse collars and ropes of all manner decorated the room. There were other objects as well, all Western-looking, but unknown to her.

"Table for three?" a harried-looking waitress in blue jeans and a bright Western shirt asked.

"Yes, please," Mike said. They followed as the woman wove her way through the crowded room to a table in another room. Tucked away from the crowd, the noise of the room behind them faded to a dull roar. They sat down, and soon the waitress returned with water and menus.

"Well, Peter, what do you want for supper?" Jenny asked, glancing over the menu. They had a children's page, and she read the list to him.

The Bargain

"Chicken." Peter decided.

"Do you want milk to drink?"

"Yeah."

The woman returned, and they placed their orders. Then they settled in to wait.

"We did real good," Mike commented. "Price-wise, it's a better year than last year was. Ranch-wise, it's the best year we've had in a long time."

"Explain that, please." Jenny leaned forward.

"We have enough hay to last through the winter this year, which we didn't have last year. The cattle are fat, and the prices are up. It's years like this that make you think ranching is a business worth being in."

"It isn't?"

"Ranching isn't a business," Mike said, carefully choosing his next words. "It's a way of life. It's a twenty-four hour a day experience. It's heartache and joy, praying and crying. In the spring, you pray for rain as the hills turn sandy. You pray for sun when you put the hay up. You pray that you make the right decisions every day – decisions that could mean life or death, going broke or staying in business. You get by on six hours of sleep a night during calving, if you're lucky. You live and die and breathe for those old cows, and then people say give the land back to the buffaloes, quit trying to feed the world. Then what do you have? Nothing. Nothing but a way of life you love and the chance to see things some people never even dream of.

"Have you ever watched a baby calf being born in the middle of a spring snowstorm when the windchill is twenty-five degrees below zero?" Mike asked. His eyes were focused on something Jenny couldn't see.

His voice lowered, and he continued, "You haven't lived until you've seen the clouds rolling in and the rain falling after a month of drought. There are some things in life that have no equal, and I've had a chance to see them. If I had a choice to do it all again, I'd choose the same again."

"All of it?" Jenny asked.

"Yeah. I'd even take the bad times back, because without them, I wouldn't see how wonderful the good times are."

They were all quiet for a long moment. Then Mike lifted his eyes and grinned sheepishly.

"I'll bet I've scared you off ranching forever."

"No." Jenny shook her head. "Quite the contrary."

Their food came, and Mike blessed it before they began eating. As Jenny cut her steak, she glanced up at the pictures along the wall. One of them was of a team of workhorses pulling a load of hay through the snow, with cows clustered around. A thought came to her, and she put her fork down, looking at Mike.

"When does feeding start?"

"Tomorrow. Well, feeding the calves in the corral starts tomorrow. You don't have to feed the cows for another few weeks."

The Bargain

"Mike, can I do it? Alone, I mean?" She asked earnestly.

"No," he said simply, "you can't."

She nodded once, then glanced down at her plate. Questions filled her mind – ones that she couldn't answer.

Mike slowly ate the last bite of his steak, swallowing before he told her what was on his mind.

"I've got an idea that might help us both."

"Yes?" Jenny looked up, wondering.

"I said that you couldn't feed alone, and that's true. But it's also true that I need help. I can feed alone, but it's not a safe practice. What if we were to help each other?"

"You mean I'd help you feed, and you would help me?"

"Yeah. Our winter ranges lie side by side, so doing that would be workable."

She went over the plan carefully in her mind, slowly smiling. "I like it. It's a wonderful idea. The only problem is you'll be doing the hard work. You'll have to make the decisions, and you'll have to teach me. It's not fair to you at all."

"Well, what if you did something more?"

"Such as?"

"What if you cooked dinner every day and let me eat with you?"

"But that's still not fair to you! Just cooking ..."

"Jenny, I'm a lousy cook. You, as I've had the fortune to discover, are a very good cook. I think it's a fair trade, but if you don't want to cook, I understand. We can think of something else."

"Actually, it isn't all that much harder to cook for three than it is to cook for two. If you think it's fair, then I agree."

"Then it's a bargain?"

"It's a bargain," Jenny agreed, shaking the hand he offered across the table.

Peter looked on with wide eyes and a happy grin. He'd get to see Mike every single day.

They finished supper, and Mike paid the bill in spite of Jenny's protests. Returning to the sale barn, they collected their checks and started home. The night was dark and moonless, the stars bright jewels scattered across the sky. Peter was asleep again, using Jenny's shoulder for a pillow. There was a silence inside the pickup broken only by a soft sigh now and then from Peter as the wheels rolled over the road in a steady rhythm.

Suddenly bright headlights arced into the cab before dimming. Jenny grabbed the arm rest on her door and clenched her teeth; the terror that filled her was as unreasonable as it was unmistakable. The other vehicle passed them, and the night became dark again, but Jenny didn't notice.

Her heart felt like it would pound through her chest any minute. Her knuckles were white, as she gripped the arm rest, and her feet pushed holes in the floor. She was screaming, yet no sound emerged. She couldn't breathe, yet she drew in a long, shuddering breath.

"What's wrong, Jenny?" Mike asked, alarmed by her reaction. He reached a hand across the cab and grasped her icy fingers in his calloused hand. "Come on, talk to me. What's going on?"

At his touch, she relaxed, the nightmare fading. She took a deep breath and tried to explain her terror.

"It's just ... ever since David's death, I've had this awful nightmare that the same thing will happen to me, and Peter will be left alone. I can't drive at night anymore, and every time I see headlights coming through the window, I get this feeling of terror, deep inside."

"Jenny, God is protecting you," Mike said gently. "Don't you know that?"

She nodded mutely.

"I'm not saying that bad things won't happen to you. But God's there when you need Him."

Mike squeezed her fingers gently before letting go.

Chapter 11

Jenny increased the throttle and maneuvered the big feeding tractor through the pasture gate, glancing back to make sure the hay sled passed through. As it moved beyond the gate, she stepped on the clutch and slid the gears into neutral to wait for Mike to shut the gate.

It was hard to believe that only four weeks ago she had sold the calves and made the bargain with Mike to share labor and food. Since then, it seemed as though she had stepped into another time and place. She was not even sure what day it was anymore, not that it mattered. Every day was the same, and every day was different. She loved it.

This morning they had finished feeding his cattle in record time. I might even make it inside in time to cook lunch by noon, Jenny thought.

After they hayed this bunch of cows, they had only the bulls and the horses left to feed. They had loaded all four sleds with hay yesterday afternoon, and that saved time today.

"OK!" Mike yelled, breaking her reverie.

The Bargain

She glanced back and saw he was standing on the tongue of the hay sled ready to go. Stepping down hard on the clutch, she put the tractor in gear and jacked the throttle up as the tractor began to move. Diesel smoke drifted up to the overcast sky, melting the few white flakes drifting into its path.

"Mommy," Peter said from his niche in the corner of the tractor cab. "I'm hungry."

"Here." She fished into her coat pocket and came up with a small pack of graham crackers. "Just one, or you'll spoil your appetite."

"OK," he agreed, taking the pack. "Where we feedin' today?"

"Mike said the same place as yesterday was fine – under the big hill. The cows will be out of the wind if it should come up."

"Oh." Peter munched on his cracker and handed the sack back.

She tucked the pack back into her pocket as she saw the trail where she needed to turn. As they approached a sharp little hill, she increased the throttle speed. She had been afraid to drive there yesterday, but today she felt confident. The tractor pulled the hay sled and several tons of hay easily up the ridge. Reaching the top, Jenny turned the tractor and headed downhill, finding the spot where they had fed the cattle yesterday. She drove north, crowding in under the steep hill. The cattle were following close enough to snitch bites of hay off the stack. Soon they would get more than a mouthful. Jenny stopped the tractor where Mike had indicated and pulled the lever that engaged the hydraulics on the hay sled. Glancing back, she saw Mike swinging up the ladder onto the hydra-fork platform. She put the tractor in gear and again looked over her shoulder at Mike. It never failed to amaze her that he could use the hydra-fork as an extension of his own arms.

The hydra-fork itself was hinged in the middle and moved with hydraulic cylinders. One end was attached to the front of the hay sled on a swivel and turned left and right. The other end was a grapple fork that opened and shut. The hydra-fork also moved up and down, and in and out. Mike used the four levers that controlled each movement and somehow made the fork move swiftly and smoothly, picking up bunch after bunch of hay and throwing it down to the cows.

The tractor hit a frozen cowpie and jolted, jerking her attention around to the front. She guided the tractor around a small hole and then glanced back at Mike.

Outside the glass windows of the tractor cab, the skies suddenly let loose a barrage of thick white flakes that swirled down on the faint breeze. Winter was on the way.

A little after noon, Jenny ladled thick soup out of the

slow cooker into bowls. Mike filled glasses with water and set them on the table before sitting down next to Peter. Jenny filled the last bowl and joined them. She bowed her head, and Mike said grace. Looking up, she handed Mike the plate of rolls.

"I'm sorry I don't have any crackers," she said.

"Your bread is so good I'll never want to eat crackers again," Mike said as he took a roll and crumbled it into his bowl.

Peter followed Mike's example, then scooped a spoonful up and blew on it.

"It's hot!" Peter exclaimed, blowing some more.

"What, you want chili to be chilly?" Mike asked. "The bread cools it just enough."

To prove his point, he took a mouthful and promptly reached for his glass of cold water.

Jenny laughed and took a more ladylike sip.

"Peter's got the right idea," Mike said. "It's good chili. How do you make it?"

"David liked his chili sweet," Jenny said. "I use a little brown sugar to tone down the chili powder. That's all."

"Mmm. It's perfect!" Mike said.

It was perfect. Cooking it in the slow cooker had been a good idea. She glanced out the kitchen windows at the snow coming down heavily now. Watching it brought to mind the question she had been meaning to ask Mike.

"Mike, do you have any plans for Thanksgiving?"

"No, not really. Because of the cattle, it's hard to get away at this time of year. Mom and Dad are planning on spending Thanksgiving with Jill and her family in Kansas City."

"Jill's your sister, right?"

"Yeah. She's got two girls. Emily is six and Beth is four. Her husband, Brian, is a doctor, and so is Jill."

"I got a turkey in town last week. We can just have our own Thanksgiving dinner after we feed."

"If you'd rather spend it alone, I don't mind."

"No!" Jenny said forcefully. "No," she said more quietly. "It would be great if you could come. We'd get lonely all by ourselves. Besides, it's hard to play any kind of game with just two people. Right, Peter?"

"Yup. Please come, Mike. Please?"

"Sounds like fun," Mike said. "Tell you what, I'll bring dessert."

"Pumpkin pie?" Jenny asked with a smile.

"Nope. You'll have to wait and see."

"Well, I guess we can wait for three more days," Jenny said, picking up her spoon again.

Thanksgiving dawned cloudy and overcast, and snow was falling. Two feet of it already covered the ground, making walking difficult. Feeding took much longer than usual. Jenny had to check the turkey at frequent intervals and then peel the potatoes to be ready to eat by one o'clock.

When Mike and Peter entered the kitchen after the feeding was done, the delicious smell of roast turkey assailed them. Gravy simmered on the stove, and a glistening turkey sat on the sideboard, golden brown and steaming. Jenny scooped stuffing into a bowl. As the door slammed, she looked up and smiled. But Mike thought he glimpsed something else in her gaze – a sad, melancholy look.

"Wash up; then we can eat," Jenny said cheerfully.

Mike padded across the floor in his stocking feet to wash at the sink. Peter was close behind.

Soon they were all seated around the dining room table. Mike looked at Jenny and Peter across the table and cleared his throat.

"In my family, we always give a special prayer on Thanksgiving. Each family member says his own thank you to the One who gives us so much all year long. Would you mind if we did that today?"

"No," Jenny said softly.

"Would you like to start, Jenny?"

"All right." She bowed her head and began quietly. "Father, thank you for this beautiful Thanksgiving Day and thank you that Mike could be with us. Thank you for our warm home and good food. Thank you for bringing us to the ranch and for such wonderful friends. In Jesus' name, Amen."

"Peter, would you like to pray next?" Mike asked when Jenny finished.

"OK. Dear God, thanks for Mike and for Mommy being here. Thanks that Mommy feels better today than she did last Thanksgiving. Thanks for takin' care of Daddy for us. Thanks too for the ranch. Amen."

"Father, thank you for Jenny and Peter. Thank you for this good food and thank you for all the blessings of the past year. Please be in our hearts and minds in the next year and continue to care for us. In Jesus' name, Amen."

Mike raised his head and reached for the knife near the turkey. Out of the corner of his eye, he saw Jenny lift a hand and wipe tears from her eyes. Questions came to mind, but he didn't voice them. Instead, he smiled at Peter.

"Well, Peter, I suppose you want the drumstick?"

Peter nodded enthusiastically.

"OK, just make sure you save room for dessert. I brought homemade chocolate ice cream."

"Yummy!" Peter held out his plate.

After dinner, Mike helped with the dishes while Peter retrieved his favorite game and set it up. Outside, the snow still fell, and Mike commented on the rarity of having so much snow so early in the year.

The Bargain

Jenny didn't answer, and he finally hung the damp dishtowel up and leaned back against the counter, crossing his arms against his chest. She finished loading the dishwasher, added soap and turned it on. Turning to rinse her hands again, she gazed out the window at the falling snow.

"It's beautiful out there," Jenny said softly.

"Yeah."

"Nothing could go wrong in a world that looks like that."

"It's a fickle world sometimes."

"Yes."

"What went wrong in your world, Jenny?"

"Sometimes everything; sometimes nothing."

"You're speaking in riddles, Jenny."

"Maybe I am."

"I'm a good listener, if you'd care to talk."

She shivered and hugged herself, gazing out at the wintry world. "I lost David a year ago last night. A year ago today my world fell apart." Tears sparkled in her eyes, and she took a deep breath. "I told myself I wasn't going to cry, not today, not now."

"Maybe it's time to cry."

At his quiet words, tears spilled out and down both cheeks, followed by a choking sob. Her hands dropped to her side, and her shoulders shook. Mike reached out to hold her, and Jenny moved close, accepting the comfort and strength his arms offered.

Teardrops seeped through his flannel shirt as he felt the pain that racked her body. There were no words to say, no kind cliches he could think of – but words weren't needed. He held her gently and let her cry.

Outside, the snow fell, hiding the hills under a blanket of white. It captured all the world in its spell, preparing it for the long winter to come. Rifts were healed as the snow quietly stole into them, covering them over.

Winter was the silence before spring, the quiet time when the earth readied itself for rebirth. Life lay dormant beneath the drifts, waiting for the first rays of sunshine, the first gentle rains, waiting for the moment when all would live and grow again. Winter was the healer.

Chapter 12

All weekend, the snow fell, gently at first, then driving down from the north on a bitter wind. Cold, frigid air carried millions of tiny ice pellets that stung the skin and numbed the body. The daily feeding became a monumental task, using the tractor to plow snow off the ground so the cattle could find the hay. Ice formed on the surface of the tanks, then became snow covered.

Jenny wrapped up as warmly as possible: layers of shirts, leggings under her jeans and finally her grandfather's heavy down-filled coat. She wrapped Peter up as well, until he was a fat bundle that could hardly walk. Still the cold crept through. It inched through all the layers and chilled them.

Struggling through the snow that would not melt, Jenny clung to Peter's hand and helped him to the pickup on Sunday morning. Mike met them with an almost cheerful grin. Jenny pulled herself in beside Peter and slammed her door. They would not be going to church today.

"Morning, Jenny. Morning, Peter. Ready to feed?"

"No," Jenny said, shivering. "This is a day not fit for man or beast."

"Well the beasts are out, and that means you've got to be too," Mike said, putting the truck in gear.

"You mean the cows?" Peter asked.

"That's right. Cows and horses ... and you!" Mike laughed.

"I'm not a beast!"

"Well – maybe not." Mike agreed. "Jenny, I'll get the tractor and head for the stack yard if you want to follow in the pickup."

"OK. Do we need to load hay today?"

"We'd better. We'll give the old girls a little extra. With some shelter and enough feed, they'll be snug as bugs in a rug."

"Did you hear the weather on the radio this morning?"

"Yep! Good news. This ought to melt some by Friday."

"That would explain your sunny mood this morning," Jenny teased.

"You'd better believe it. As soon as those roads clear, we're going to town."

"Town?"

"For groceries. The way this winter's starting, I don't

want to be caught in a blizzard with an empty larder." On that note, Mike left the pickup to start the tractor. Jenny watched the tractor back out of the shop, its chains crunching through the snow. She drove the pickup on the path the tractor blazed to the stack yard to load feed for another day.

Jenny awoke before dawn on Friday morning. Thursday had been clear; the sun had shone so brightly on the snow that the whole world glittered. Mike had called neighbors who lived closer to the highway and discovered that the roads were open all the way to Ogallala.

Last night, they had fed extra hay, so all they needed to do was feed cottonseed cake and chop ice on the tanks before leaving for town. Jenny made a grocery list to outdo all lists. As long as there was room enough in the pickup, they would be all right.

If I hurry, I'll have time to wash and dry my hair before Mike comes, Jenny thought. She ran the water and unbraided her hair. What can I get Peter for Christmas? How will I get it home unseen?

It was shortly before noon when Mike, Jenny and Peter drove into Ogallala.

The Bargain

It seemed as though the whole town had turned into a Christmas village. Tinsel decorations were hung from light poles. Store windows were painted with snowy scenes. The church on Main Street had a Nativity out in front. Strains of Christmas carols drifted through the streets.

They ate an early lunch. Then Mike took Jenny and Peter to a farm and ranch supply store near the sale barn. Jenny stomped the snow from her boots before following Mike and Peter inside. Mike circled around the checkout counters and stopped in the clothing department where racks of women's clothing crowded the small space.

"Come on," Mike urged as Jenny lagged behind.

"What are you buying here?" she asked.

"Your Christmas present," Mike said, leading her toward the rack on the back wall. It was filled with Arctic-weight coveralls made from heavy, brown-duck material with a quilted lining.

"What are these?"

"Something to keep you warm this winter. Let's find a pair that fits." He reached into the rack and pulled out a pair, holding them up to Jenny. "What about these?"

"Sure, if there were two of me." She laughed.

She pulled a smaller pair off the rack and soon found a pair that fit. The coveralls zipped up the front and from the knees down the outer seams of the legs, allowing them to be put on over a pair of snow boots.

"Good!" Mike said in satisfaction. "You'll be warm enough all winter. I just wish they had them in Peter's size."

"Speaking of Peter ..." Jenny's voice trailed off, as she glanced around. "Where is he?"

"I don't know." Mike grabbed the coveralls, threw them over one arm and began walking quickly down the aisle.

"Peter!" Jenny called, following Mike.

They jogged down aisles crowded with Christmas merchandise, but neither of them saw any sign of Peter until they rounded the last one. Standing there, gazing at rows of green and red toy tractors, was Peter. Relieved, Jenny knelt down beside him, and he turned to face her.

"See, Mommy. It's a tractor just like Mike's!" He grinned and pointed. Jenny never took her eyes from his face.

"Honey, you can't just wander away like that. You scared me half to death."

His happy smile was suddenly replaced by a worried frown.

"I'm sorry. Just ... saw these, and you were busy."

"That's all right, honey." She wrapped her arms around him and hugged him close. Then she drew away and looked him in the eyes. "Just don't do it again, OK?"

"OK, Mommy."

The Bargain

"Now, where's that tractor that looks just like Mike's?"

After they finished shopping, Mike took Peter out to the pickup, and Jenny took her purchases to the checkout counter. The tractor that Peter had liked so much was among them, along with a horse trailer and some plastic cattle and horses appropriately sized. There was also a pair of snow boots Peter's size, and another pair her size. Both had leather uppers, rubber soles and removable liners. The boots were guaranteed warm to forty degrees below zero. She and Peter would be ready for winter.

"Next stop, the grocery store," Mike said as he helped her load sacks behind the pickup seat.

"Sounds good to me."

Peter was quiet as they drove to the grocery store. Inside, he clung close to Jenny. She and Mike each took a cart and dug lists out of their pockets.

An hour and a half later, the last sack of groceries was loaded into the back of the pickup, and the grocery boy had hauled the carts inside. Jenny peered through the back window, making sure that everything was well-situated for the ride home.

Doubt rose in her as she surveyed the load. I can't use this many groceries in a lifetime, much less in five months, she thought. There were staples – three hundred pounds of flour, fifty pounds of white sugar, sacks of brown sugar, salt, dozens of eggs and boxes of margarine. And there were extras – canned vegetables and fruits, juice, and dozens of other items. The bill had seemed astronomical, but Mike had assured her it was bound to be cheaper than going to town every week.

He turned the pickup into the street, then pulled onto a side street.

"There's one more stop I've got to make," he said. "You two wait here; it'll only take a minute."

"Sure."

Mike got out and hurried down an alley toward the main street. Jenny looked out the window at the quiet neighborhood decorated for the holiday and hummed a carol under her breath.

"Mommy?"

"What, honey?"

"Is it Christmas again?"

"Almost. You know that. We talked about it the other night."

"I know. But, Mommy, will we have a real Christmas this time?"

"What do you mean?"

"Not like last time, but a real Christmas."

The Bargain

Last time – last year, he meant. No, last year had not been a real Christmas at all. There had been a gift for Peter and church services on Christmas morning, but it had not been a child's Christmas – the kind that remained in a youngster's mind as a joyful experience.

She still mourned for David. But was remembering the way it used to be going to make Peter feel better? She resolved at that moment that Peter would have a real Christmas, even if she had to chop down a tree and sing carols with a sore throat. Christmas was Jesus' birthday, and they should celebrate it as such.

"Yes, honey, it's going to be a real Christmas. I promise."

Just then Mike hurried back, clutching a small sack in one hand. As he got in, he tucked it into the side pocket of his door and started the truck.

"Sorry it took so long," he said as he checked his mirrors.

"You were very quick," Jenny assured him.

"Good." Mike glanced over at Peter. "Hey, Peter, what's that smile all over your face? Who said you could smile?"

At this jesting, Peter grinned more.

"Mommy said we could have a real Christmas this year." He shifted his attention to Jenny. "Mommy, can Mike come to Christmas?"

"If he wants to, but he has to like homemade fudge. We can't eat a whole batch by ourselves."

"With a bargain like that, who could say no?" Mike grinned and started driving out of town. He reached over and turned on the radio.

"... and I've brought some corn for popping ... The lights are turned way down low. Let it snow, let it snow, let it snow ..."

The song echoed cheerfully in the confines of the pickup. Jenny and Mike both joined in the chorus, with Peter singing along behind them. Above, the afternoon skies had clouded over, and a few snowflakes whirled down. The singers were about to get their wish.

Mike flicked the headlights on, and Peter settled in for the long ride home. Only Jenny remained detached, apart. She gazed out the side window and said a silent prayer that God would help her put her whole heart into Christmas. As the snow began falling thickly, she felt her spirits rise. Yes, it was going to be a wonderful Christmas. Thank you, Father.

Chapter 13

On Christmas Eve, the aroma of baking cookies filled the house as snow slanted against the north windows. Jenny added drops of red coloring to a small bowl of frosting and set it on the kitchen table near Peter. He was laboriously applying green frosting to a sugar cookie and barely glanced up when she left the kitchen.

A real Christmas? If baking and decorating counted, Jenny was doing fine. In the attic she had found a tall, artificial tree and boxes of decorations and lights. Now the tree sat resplendent in the living room, tiny colored lights, nestled among the branches, blinking on and off. Delicate colored balls and family heirlooms were mixed with Peter's cookie-cutter, salt-dough ornaments. An angel topped the tree.

An evergreen garland, held in place by red velvet bows, decorated the banister, all the way up the stairs. Crocheted snowflakes hung by string in the windows – not that they needed any reminder of snow – and stockings hung in front of the fireplace. Best of all, Grandma's Nativity set sat on the mantle. Baby Jesus was surrounded by shepherds, wise men and loving parents.

Jenny changed the tape of carols in the tape player and hurried back to the kitchen as the timer rang, signaling that the last cookies were done. Grabbing pot holders, she pulled the pans from the oven and scooped the cookies onto a rack. Peter had started on the red frosting and was delicately adding sprinkles to a snowflake.

"That's pretty," Jenny said, looking across the table before putting the pans in the sink.

"Look at that one." Peter pointed to another cookie on the tray.

"Very nice! You're doing a good job. Do you want me to help?"

"OK."

She sat down next to him and picked up a cookie. They worked silently for a few minutes, then Peter carefully placed his finished cookie on the tray and looked up.

"When's Mike comin', Mommy?"

"At five." Jenny glanced at the clock. "In an hour."

"Goody!" Peter grinned. "Can I give him my present?"

"Yes, you may." She grinned as she recalled the special gift Peter was going to give Mike.

"We done?" Peter asked.

"Mmm hmm." She added frosting to the last cookie

as Peter jumped down from his chair. "Wash your hands, and then you can go play if you want to."

Peter skipped out of the kitchen as Jenny finished the last cookie. She got the meat thermometer and checked on the ham in the oven before cleaning off the table and starting to wash the dishes.

Mike grabbed a box off the pickup seat and balanced an awkward bundle on top before slamming the door shut. He bowed his head against the wind as he trudged toward Jenny's house. The light from the windows looked warm and welcoming. Reaching the back door, he knocked.

"Come in!" Jenny called from the kitchen.

"I'm in!" Mike answered, as he set the box on the washer. He piled his hat, mittens, coat and coveralls on the floor before taking off his snow boots.

The door between the kitchen and the porch had a festive wreath, welcoming him into the house. As he walked through the door, he glanced up. Peter had insisted on hanging up the plastic mistletoe he'd found in the attic.

When Jenny asked him why, he'd said, "Because Christmas is when everybody loves everybody else. When I see the mistletoe, I remember that."

Jenny was dressed in jeans and a pretty red and green

plaid shirt that sparkled with gold threads.

"Something smells good," Mike said, as he shut the door.

"I hope you're hungry." She laughed, carrying a platter of ham to the dining room table.

"I brought some gifts."

She turned to face him, mock disapproval in her eyes. "You didn't have to. However, since you did, I guess you'll just have to put them under the tree like everyone else." Her face lit up with a sweet smile, and he smiled back.

"I can handle that."

Mike returned to the porch for his box and carried it into the living room. Adding several colorful bundles and one huge package to the pile beneath the tree, he realized that he hadn't felt as homesick this year as usual. He remembered the gift he had gotten for Jenny. Then he began wondering if he would ever be able to give it to her?

"Mike!" Peter's excited cry rang out as he thundered down the stairs.

"Hey, Peter! Ready for Christmas?"

"Yup! I even made you a present. Want to see it?"

"Better not, just yet. Your mom won't like it if we skip supper and just open presents."

"What won't Mom like?" Jenny asked as she entered the room.

"I was just telling Peter we'd better do justice to the

feast you've prepared before we begin rippping into the packages."

Mike gave Peter a big wink.

"Well, thank you. Time to wash up; supper's on," Jenny said.

Mike looked the table over and marveled at the feast before him. Ham, crackers and cheeses of all kinds, apple slices, oranges, cranberry sauce, fresh rolls, salads, and three pies. He sighed and looked down at his plate. If he worked his way through this before midnight, it would be amazing. Picking up his fork, he started in.

"This is really good," he said after a bite of fluffy pink salad.

"Thank you. Laurie gave me the recipe over the phone last night."

"Oh yeah? How are they?"

"The Christmas Eve service at the church was canceled because most of the congregation can't get there. The roads are drifted shut again, and the county won't take the snow blower out on Christmas Eve. Jimmy has not been to school since Thanksgiving. Other than that, they're doing well."

"I've never seen the roads this snowy," Mike said. "They've been bad before, but they were always cleared off right away. I heard that the snow is piled so high there's nowhere to put it. Now part of the road between here and the highway is running through somebody's pasture, and it has snow walls five feet high.

"It's a good thing we got to town when we did," Jenny agreed. "It certainly has given us a white Christmas."

After supper, Jenny and Mike put the leftover food away. Then Jenny read the Christmas story aloud.

Mike found himself watching Peter. The familiar story became new and exciting as the little boy listened. He beamed when Jenny read about the shepherds and the angels. In Peter's eyes, Mike clearly saw a baby being born in the barn with sweet-smelling hay for a bed. When Jenny finished, they were all quiet, envisioning God himself as a child born among the lowest of beasts.

Peter was the first to break the silence. He pointed a finger toward the tree and asked, "Can I give Mike his present, Mommy?"

"All right," Jenny said, as she laid the Bible aside.

Peter ran to the tree, found a lumpy, child-wrapped present and gave it to Mike with a dramatic flourish.

Mike patted the couch beside him, and Peter sat down, watching eagerly while Mike opened it. Mike held up a small crate made out of ice-cream sticks.

"I made it!" Peter exclaimed.

"You did? It's just what I need to hold all the stuff

that comes out of my pockets."

Peter grinned, then hopped off the couch and ran toward the pile of gifts Jenny had made for him on the floor. Jenny and Mike watched as Peter enthusiastically tore into the first gift.

Soon, he had paper strewn all over the floor, along with his tractor and animals. Only the bulky gift from Mike remained unopened. Mike caught Jenny's puzzled expression as Peter reached for it. Four feet long and two feet wide, it was bigger than Peter.

Peter ripped the paper off with abandon and cried out with joy. Before him lay a toboggan, with a gleaming wood finish, a curved front and rope handle.

"Wow! A sled!"

"Mike, you shouldn't have."

"Well, I was going to get a puppy," Mike said with an impish grin.

"The sled's beautiful!" Jenny hastily amended.

As Peter sat on his sled, Jenny brought the remaining gifts to the couch. Most of them were for Mike. There were three for Jenny, and she looked at him questioningly.

"Go ahead," he urged.

The first was a pretty dusky-blue and rose-plaid flannel shirt. There was also a tooled leather belt and a framed aerial photograph of the house and valley.

"You already gave me the coveralls ..."

"My mom made the shirt, and Jill got you the belt. A

guy who came through here last year took the picture. I got it, thinking I'd give it to your grandfather for Christmas."

"Thank you. You'll have to give me their addresses, and I'll be sure to thank them."

"You bet."

Jenny looked again at the picture on her lap. "It's beautiful," she whispered.

"Glad you like it. Can I open my presents now?" Mike asked, hoping she wouldn't cry.

"Go ahead." She stroked the soft flannel shirt with a finger and glanced over as he opened his present from her.

Mike dropped the paper on the floor and spread out the soft folds of a brightly colored afghan.

"Did you make this?"

"Yes. I finished it last night."

"When did you find the time?"

"I started on it the weekend after we went to town, and I just worked on it when I could. Do you really like it?"

"It's perfect!" Mike proclaimed, holding it up. "It'll come in handy on those cold winter nights."

"Good!" Jenny smiled, placing her gifts on the coffee table. "I'll go get us some cocoa and candy, and then you can find out what's in the other packages for you."

Mike reached for the present from his mother and father. But he couldn't help wondering how anything could compare with what he had just received – a gift of time, energy, patience and friendship. It was just as well that the rest of his gifts were warm shirts and blue jeans. He put them in the box almost as quickly as he opened them. He made room on the couch for Jenny as she returned.

Jenny came down from tucking Peter in bed and saw that Mike had cleaned up the living room. He carefully folded the afghan and put it into a box. Jenny picked up the plate of candy and the empty mugs and carried them to the kitchen. Mike was close behind, carrying his gifts. As she rinsed the cups, she heard him wrapping up against the weather. She moved to the doorway as he zipped up his coat.

"Thank you for coming tonight and for bringing everything. Peter loved the sled. We'll have to try it out tomorrow."

"Sure. Thank you for letting me come. It was fun ... really fun, Jenny."

Mike stepped toward her. He gently brushed a wayward lock of hair from her brow and touched his lips to her forehead in a hint of a kiss. Stepping back, he picked up his box.

"Good night, Jenny. Merry Christmas." Then he was gone.

The Bargain

She stood staring at the door long after the sound of his pickup had died away. Why had Mike done that? It had been so brief, so fleeting, that she wondered if perhaps she had imagined it. But she knew she hadn't.

Reaching up, she flicked the light off and started to shut the door, but something caught, preventing the door from shutting. She reached up to free it then stopped. In the soft kitchen light, the plastic sprig of mistletoe seemed almost real as she finished closing the door.

The next afternoon, Jenny and Mike took Peter sledding on his toboggan. They chose a gentle slope and used the tractor to pack the snow. When the path was smooth, Mike parked the tractor and returned to where Jenny and Peter stood with the sled.

"Ready?"

Peter grinned and nodded.

"Well, don't just stand there! Let's go sledding."

Mike grabbed the rope handle and pulled the sled to the top of the hill. Peter and Jenny followed.

Mike turned the sled around and motioned for Peter to get on in front, then he climbed on behind, grabbing the rope.

"Here we go!" Mike shouted as the sled began to move. Jenny watched as it slid down the hill, Peter clinging tightly to the front and laughing. It passed beyond the slope of the hill and traveled halfway up the next before coming to a stop.

"Wow!" Peter's excited chatter drifted to her ears. "Mommy, did you see that?"

She nodded and smiled as they dragged the sled up the hill again. The next time, Peter rode by himself, and Mike cheered him on from the top. The ride after that, Peter insisted Mike join him.

"We go faster with you," Peter said.

So Mike went. Three more rides passed before Peter suddenly noticed Jenny standing on the hill.

"Mommy, you go this time," Peter said, as Mike brought the sled up the hill again. "I want to make a snow angel."

"You can go, Peter."

"No, you go, Mommy."

"It's just ... I've never been sledding before." Jenny admitted.

"Never?" Peter asked, open-mouthed.

"Never?" Mike mimicked in shocked amazement.

"Nope. Not even when I was a little girl."

"That's terrible! I never did 'til today, but I'm still little, and you're really old. You got to go, Mommy!"

"Yeah!" Mike said.

"I don't know how," Jenny explained.

"You're never too old to learn something new, even if you are really old," Mike said with finality. "Come on."

The Bargain

Before she knew it, Jenny was in the front of the sled, grasping the curved front tightly. The hill suddenly seemed much steeper. Mike was behind her, and she felt his arms encircle her as he reached to grasp both sides of the front to help steer.

"Ready?" he asked, his voice near her ear.

"Go!" she shouted, and he pushed off the top of the hill.

Suddenly they were flying, snow spraying up in her face. Faster and faster they went, and then time paused. She began laughing. Behind them, Peter cheered loudly.

They reached the bottom of the hill too soon, but the sled didn't stop. It bumped up on the next hill, then slid sideways and stopped.

Jenny spilled onto the snowy hillside as the sled turned. Laughing and gasping, she lay still. Conscious of a thousand things, she looked at the milky blue sky and the snow-encrusted world that surrounded her.

Mike had landed beside her, on his stomach. She giggled at his appearance as he rose to his hands and knees.

"You're Frosty the Snowman!" She laughed.

"And you're very rude to laugh at a man when he's down," Mike said in feigned solemnity.

"I can't help it."

Climbing to her feet, she dusted herself off and grabbed the rope on the sled before starting up the hill again.

"Do you mind if I ride with Peter next time?" she called back to Mike.

"Not at all." It was enough just to see her laugh again, but he didn't tell her that.

Chapter 14

Christmas gave way to January – a more icy, snowy January than anyone could remember. In the middle of the month, Mike and Jenny moved both cow herds into the most protected pasture and fed a stack of hay every day under the hill.

"Desperate times call for desperate measures," Mike said in jest, as they loaded a haystack on the sled one morning.

He may have been joking, but winter was serious. Three feet of snow made every step, every move, a fight. The blades on the fronts of the tractors came into use like never before, pushing away snow so the cattle could find feed and water.

The weather dropped below zero and remained there. The wind sometimes brought the temperature down to twenty below. Every day was a struggle. Even Peter was affected. He became quiet and listless. Had there been some way to leave him in the house safely and spare him the cold, Jenny would have done it. As it was, Peter was bundled into a vehicle each day. Mike and Jenny let Peter choose whether to ride in the tractor with Jenny or in the pickup with Mike.

Jenny increased the throttle on the tractor and pulled out of the stack yard, dropping the blade and pushing the latest accumulation of snow to the side. She could not see around the snowy stack on the sled, but she knew that Mike and Peter were close behind in the pickup.

Mike and Peter ... she looked up at the overcast sky spilling snow and wondered at the warmth that rose in her when she thought of them. Mike was a part of their lives that was difficult to define. He and Peter were the best of friends and ....

Her train of thought was interrupted as she came to the pasture gate. Bringing the tractor to a halt, she opened the door, climbed down and waded through deep snow to the gate. She dragged it wide and struggled back to the tractor. Her snow boots felt like lead weights as she climbed back into the cab and drove into the pasture.

Just past the gate, the view of the hills and sky suddenly disappeared as the snow wrapped the tractor in a swirling gray blanket. Panic rose in her throat and she glanced back, unable even to see the stack she pulled behind her. The wind shrieked and howled. Jenny reached to step on the clutch. Then she realized that if she stopped and Mike didn't, he would run into the back of the sled.

"Help me, Father!" She cried out, staring into the storm. "Lord, I can't even see the hills."

As the wind blew, Jenny remembered a Bible story about the prophet Elijah. He had felt despair, and the Lord told him to stand on the mountain, for the Lord would soon pass by. A powerful wind tore the mountains apart and shattered the rocks, but the Lord was not in the wind. There was an earthquake and a fire, but God had not been in them either. God had been the still, small whisper that came after it all.

"I'm listening, God. Just tell me what to do," Jenny whispered. A peace that belied the moment enveloped her.

Minutes passed like hours, then suddenly the storm lifted, and Jenny saw that she had followed the trail right to the cattle. She stopped, and moments later, Mike rounded the stack and pulled the door open.

"That was a scary little blizzard back there," he said. "I was close enough to see the back of the sled, and when it didn't stop, I just kept following."

"I didn't know what to do. I didn't want you to run into me, so I just kept going," Jenny said.

"It worked." Mike grinned, but only his mouth showed between his dark snow glasses and coat collar. "Ready to feed?"

The Bargain

"I'll grade a path through to the other side."

"OK." He leapt out of the cab, then called back, "I was praying for you!"

"I know." It was her turn to smile, and as she swung the door shut and started the tractor moving through the cattle, she felt a new warmth rising in her for this man. He was a good friend, she decided, a very good friend.

A month passed, February's weather conditions were no different than January's, but it was a month closer to spring. Flipping the calendar, Jenny began marking off the days, trying to keep her sanity. The roads were packed with snow, leaving Jenny, Mike and Peter stranded and facing another monotonous week.

Monday came, and Jenny felt her temper grow short. Even the promise of reading a new book aloud to Peter that afternoon didn't cheer her up as it usually did. She was quiet as they fed the cattle, pushing the restlessness away as much as she could.

At dinner, Mike complimented her on the meat loaf and baked potatoes, saying, "This is just as good as yesterday's was."

"I cooked this yesterday?" she asked.

"Yeah, Mommy, with green beans," Peter said.

"I cooked the same meal two days in a row? No, I

couldn't have."

"That's OK, Mommy. I like meat loaf and 'taters."

"It's not just that. It's everything. I'm living the same day over and over, and we're having meat loaf every time. How could I do that? How could this be happening? I used to be sane."

Peter and Mike both looked up, startled at the outburst.

"I'm sorry; I really am. There was no call to answer like that. It's just ..."

"Every day is the same," Mike finished for her.

"Yes. How do you keep from going crazy?"

"I look forward to dinner. It's different every day – almost." Mike grinned.

Wavering between laughter and tears, Jenny opted for laughter and reached for the salt.

That afternoon, Jenny was startled at a knock on the door, and Mike stuck his head in.

"Get your wraps," He ordered.

"What?"

"Wrap up. You too, Peter," Mike said, pulling their coats and snow pants off the porch rack. "We're going to have an outing."

"An outing?"

"Just wrap up."

The Bargain

Five minutes later, both Peter and Jenny were in Mike's pickup, the good one that he drove to town. He shifted into four-wheel drive, and all four tires gripped the road as they left the yard. When they got to the main road, Jenny smiled.

"They plowed the road!"

Forty minutes later, Mike turned onto a freshly plowed side road. They wound through the hills and finally came to a stop in front of Frank and Laurie Richards' house. Jenny got out and helped Peter down.

She hurried to the front door and knocked gently.

"Jenny!" Laurie said, surprise mixed with delight when she answered the door.

"Oh, Laurie, it's so good to see you."

"Come in." Laurie pulled her inside and hugged her close, ignoring the snowy outer layers Jenny wore.

Jenny joined Laurie in the kitchen, and they hugged again.

"Mike said we were going on an outing. I never guessed he meant here until he turned off the road."

"Frank told me to clean the house, but he didn't say why. Oh, it's so good to see you; I've had cabin fever all week."

"Me too. Can you believe it? I cooked the same meal two days in a row."

They laughed together, and suddenly the world was right again. The snow melted from their minds as they talked about everything that had happened during the snowbound weeks.

It was late when they finally got home. Mike carried a sleeping Peter into the house and upstairs. Jenny helped Peter into his pajamas before letting him tumble into bed. Returning downstairs, she saw Mike hanging up Peter's coat.

"Thank you so much for today," she said softly.

"We all needed a break. Calving will start pretty soon, and we won't have time for anything then."

"Thank you just the same. You're a good friend." Stepping forward, Jenny hugged Mike quickly, then hurried back into the kitchen.

He stared after her for a moment before reaching for the door and stepping into the cold night. Outside, he paused a moment. There was a hint of snow in the wind again. Would this winter ever end?

March came in like a lion, teeth bared and growling as a blizzard swept the hills. On March 21st, Jenny and Mike began readying the calving barn. They set panels up, forming small stalls in the long metal building. Hay a foot thick carpeted the floor. Mike put new bulbs in the sockets that ran the length of the building and checked the tall corral lights. Finally, they moved the pregnant heifers into the sheltered lot behind the barn, and Mike began teaching Jenny how to check the cows.

Soon the pregnant cows and heifers would have to be checked every few hours all night long. Should a cow begin to calve, she would have to be moved to the barn to have her baby in a dry place.

As the days passed, Jenny watched the cows grow heavy. With anxious eyes, she watched the weather. How could any mother-to-be survive this bitter cold? Then one morning, the calving season officially began.

"Mommy, what's that cow looking for?" Peter asked from his seat in the tractor.

"I don't know. Which cow?"

Peter pointed. "There, that one, with the funny balloon on her tail. How come she's sniffing the ground?"

"Oh boy," Jenny muttered. She stuck her head out the door of the tractor and yelled up at Mike, who was pitching hay with the hydra-fork.

"Mike?"

"Yeah?"

"We've got a problem."

She pointed, and he nodded.

"That's not a problem; that's calving." He grinned. "We'll take her in when we finish up here."

Then he turned back to the hay, leaving a nervous Jenny and a captivated Peter. A baby was coming. The first of four hundred babies was about to make its way into the frozen world.

Chapter 15

The alarm clock's incessant ringing brought Jenny to consciousness again. Reaching out a hand, she turned it off and rolled to the edge of the bed, swinging her legs to the floor. The red digital numbers on the clock read 1:55 a.m. – time for her to check the cows.

Mustering the strength to stand, she checked on Peter. He was breathing evenly, deep in sleep. Leaving him, she made her way to the kitchen in the darkness. Flicking on the kitchen light, she blinked at the sudden glare. As her eyes adjusted, she moved a pile of wraps off the chair and sat down, reaching for her coveralls.

She pulled them on over the fleecy sweat suit she wore to bed and zipped them up. Sticking her sock-covered feet in heavy snow boots, she tied them and pulled the coverall legs down over their tops. Grabbing her coat, she pulled it on. Then she jammed the cap with the ear flaps on her head and picked up her fleece-lined leather mittens.

Glancing at the table, she saw that Mike hadn't left a note from the midnight check. There must not have been any babies coming. Maybe there wouldn't be any coming now, either.

She grabbed the big flashlight off the cupboard and reached for the porch door. The sooner she went out, the sooner she would be back. Maybe she could get an hour's sleep before the four o'clock shift. Still, she was blessed. If she and Mike hadn't teamed up she might be checking all night long instead of just on the early morning shift. She got to sleep every night until two o'clock. If she got Peter to bed by eight, she got six hours of sleep in a row, then some catnaps. It worked out evenly though. Mike got catnaps, then six hours of sleep before breakfast.

Flicking the flashlight on, she stepped onto the porch. She turned the light on and then reached for the door knob. Suddenly, the door was jerked open. She stepped back in surprise, her eyes taking in the snowy creature before her.

"Mike! What's wrong?"

"Got a calf here." He half turned, and she saw that the filthy bundle in his arms was a calf.

"Come in," she said, stepping aside. He walked inside, and she shut the door against the cold. Gently lowering the calf to the floor, he looked up.

"You got an old blanket or a rag or something?"

"Just a minute." She ran to the pantry and grabbed an old wool blanket off the bottom shelf.

"Here," she said, handing it to him.

Mike began rubbing the calf briskly, drying the slimy, cold, wet hide. The calf lay limp, its eyes shut. The tiniest movement of its nostrils were all that indicated it was alive.

"What happened to him?"

"That bonehead of a cow," Mike said between clenched teeth, "must have had him after I went out at ten. She left the hill and headed for the windiest, most snowy hill in the pasture. Then she had her calf and left him shivering in a snow bank while she headed back for the warm hay."

"How awful," Jenny said.

"Any longer out there and he'd have been dead. I saw the cow standing at the end of the herd and noticed she'd calved, but I couldn't find the calf. I followed a hunch and looked for trails that led out of the hollow. Sure enough, she'd left him in a snowdrift."

"Your cow or mine?"

"I don't know, but she's going to the sale barn before calving next year. We don't have to put up with this kind of behavior."

"How could any creature do that?"

"I don't know." Mike shook his head, some of the fire fading from his eyes. "Just not very smart."

"No." Jenny shook her head and looked down at the baby. Mike had him almost dry. He gave another few good rubs and leaned back.

"I don't know if he'll be alive in the morning, but

we've done what we could." He wrapped the dry portion of the blanket around the calf and stood up. "We'll leave him here for tonight. Tomorrow will tell."

"Today, you mean," Jenny said with a tired smile. "You'd better get home and get some sleep. I'll go run through the herd and see if anything else is happening. Don't worry about getting out too early tomorrow. I'll have breakfast ready at seven, so come by whenever you can."

"Thanks, Jenny." His face was haggard, but his gratitude heartfelt.

"Just get some sleep. Say a prayer for the calf, and leave him in God's hands. It's all anyone can do now," she said as they stepped outside.

"Good night, Jenny."

"Good night, Mike."

She waited until he had left, then she walked to the shed where her pickup was parked. She unplugged it, backed out of the garage and headed for the pasture. As she approached the cattle, she switched the spotlight on and held it out the window, playing it over the herd. The heavy black cows were laying comfortably in the hay in the lee of the hill, chewing their cud.

Assured that nothing was happening in the big pasture, Jenny moved on. Walking through the lot where the heifers were, she saw nothing there either. After glancing in the barn at the four mamas and babies Mike had run in earlier, she returned to the house. Going inside, Jenny took a quick look at the limp baby calf. Then she checked on Peter and returned to bed, setting the clock to go off in an hour for the 4 o'clock check.

As she drifted off to sleep, Jenny thought wryly that maybe there was a reason why she felt tired all the time.

Returning to the house, Jenny glanced at the clock – it was a little after six. During the four o'clock check, there had been a steady stream of calves. She'd got one into the barn and had to return and get another one ... then a third and fourth. Finally things had slowed. Running one last check just before coming in, Jenny found that everything had been quiet. Now it was time to start breakfast. Soon, Peter would be up and about, ready for the day.

She mixed up biscuits, scrambled eggs and was setting the table when a knock sounded on the door and Mike came in. Her heartbeat quickened at his familiar figure. She looked up and smiled as he leaned against the doorjamb.

"Morning, Jenny."

"Good morning. Breakfast will be ready in a few minutes."

"It smells good." Glancing back onto the porch, he asked, "Did you have to haul the calf out?"

"The calf? I didn't do anything with the calf." Jenny

dropped the silverware on the table with a clatter and hurried to the porch after Mike.

"There's the little fella." Mike laughed.

Standing on wobbly legs, the calf was behind the coat rack, looking around.

"Maa!" he called, tipping his head back and looking at them with big brown eyes.

"Look at him," Jenny laughed, delight welling up within her.

"I thought he was a goner. Just look at him now," Mike crowed.

They both watched the little miracle that had happened in the night with wonder and awe.

"This ... this makes everything worth doing," Mike said softly.

"Yes, it does," Jenny agreed quietly.

A slightly scorched smell drifted to the porch, and the spell was broken.

"The eggs!" Jenny cried, running for the stove.

Startled, the calf wobbled back a step, running into a metal bucket that dropped to the floor with a clang. Mike went to rescue the calf, and Jenny called Peter for breakfast.

Mike dropped into his easy chair one afternoon and closed his eyes. But he found he couldn't sleep. All he could think about was that he was in love with Jenny and she didn't know it. Maybe he was crazy, but he couldn't stop thinking of her. She thought of him only as a friend. He recalled her impulsive little hug the day he took her to see Laurie and her words – "You're a good friend, Mike."

"Yeah, I'm a friend. What if I wanted to be more?"

With a sigh, he reached for his Bible on the stand beside the chair. It fell open, and he glanced at the page. Proverbs 17:17 caught his eye, and he read aloud, "A friend loves at all times, and a brother is born for adversity."

Loves at all times, huh? Well, that much was true. Flipping to the next page, his eyes fell on verse 18:22, "He who finds a wife finds what is good and receives favor from the Lord."

"God, I'm giving this matter over to You," Mike said. "If it's Your will that Jenny become my wife, then let it be. If not, then let me be her friend. In Your name, Amen."

A small measure of comfort came then, and while he did not dismiss her from his mind, he was able to sleep.

Jenny curled up on the couch under an afghan and closed her eyes. She was so tired. A nap was a wonderful idea. Her body relaxed, and she willed her mind to be silent as well. Unguarded thoughts pushed forward though, bringing to light something she had been trying to ignore. Could she be falling in love with Mike? Guilt assailed her, reminding her of all the times she'd said she'd never love again.

She thought of David, a thought that three months ago would have brought a pang to her heart and tears to her eyes. Memories came like photographs, crystal-clear moments that would remain with her forever: their wedding day, David's infectious laugh, riding the ferry in the rain, Peter's birth, David holding their child. There had been so many good times.

How could she think romantically of Mike? She pushed the thoughts away once again and rolled over. Sleep claimed her before she could think any more, but she could not deny what she felt.

Chapter 16

Mike snapped on the ear tagger, and the calf became red tag number 182. Jenny scribbled the number of the calf and the number of the bawling cow in the small black book, and Mike turned the calf out into the pasture. The cow rushed to the calf's side and sniffed it carefully. The calf followed as the cow trotted toward the windmill.

"How many to go?" Mike asked, closing the gate behind the pair.

"Yet to calve, you mean? Well yesterday, the last day of April, you had eighteen and I had twenty-two. Minus two each, means you've got sixteen, and I've got twenty."

"I'm going to be done before you are." Mike grinned.

"I wouldn't be too sure of that. Babies come when they're ready."

"Whatever. The important thing is that calving season is almost over."

"Spring is the most important thing," Jenny said as she looked around her.

The Bargain

The hills were brown with a tinge of green. All that remained of the long winter were white patches of snow in small hollows hidden from the sun. The wind was warm; the sun shone bright; and a cheery, yellow-breasted western meadowlark warbled his flute-like song from a nearby fence post. Everywhere, spring was coming, poking its head up as cautiously as the grass in the meadow. One day, only a few brave sprigs were showing; the next, the entire meadow was engulfed in a wave of green.

The cows and calves had been sorted gradually into their respective pastures after the snow began to melt. Only the heavy cows remained together in the lot behind Jenny's barn, waiting until they too had their calves.

"This is the last to haul out today, isn't it?" Mike asked.

"Mmm hmm. All the babies are out of the barn and the pasture. Now we can finish feeding, then we can clean the barn."

"Oh ..." He groaned.

"Remember those long, cold nights when the barn was full? Today there are only four stalls that we have to clean."

"That does put a perspective on things."

"Besides." She smiled winningly. "I made chocolate cake for dinner. That will give you plenty of energy to clean the barn."

"You win again," he said, getting in the pickup. "Let's go."

With a last glance at the cow and calf now some ways off, Jenny crawled in the pickup and handed the calf book to Mike, who stuffed it in his shirt pocket before starting the engine.

"Wore the little feller out, didn't we?" Mike said, glancing at Peter asleep in the middle of the seat.

"I don't think he feels well. I should have left him inside this morning, but I hate to leave him alone in the house."

Jenny placed her hand on his flushed forehead, a worried look in her eyes.

"He looks pretty comfortable." Mike shrugged. "Let's just leave him in the pickup while we feed. There's no sense putting him in the tractor if he feels bad."

"All right."

A few moments later, Mike pulled up in front of the stack-yard gate. Jenny jumped out and opened it. Mike drove through and parked. The tractor was hooked to the sled and ready to go. Mike got out of the pickup and walked toward the tractor.

"We have enough hay?" Jenny asked joining him.

"Yeah. You bring the pickup, and I'll start for the flat just north of the windmill in the cow-calf pasture."

"Sure." She turned toward the pickup.

Behind her, Jenny heard the tractor start, the familiar diesel engine winding up as Mike started through the gate with three tons of hay. In the pasture, a cow's head came up. Spring may have come, but feeding went on. Feeding would continue until the grass in the pasture could sustain the cows. But it was the first of May, so it would only be a little longer.

Jenny tucked Peter into bed for the afternoon. He hadn't been able to keep his lunch down.

"Is he going to be OK?" Mike asked when Jenny came downstairs.

"He ought to be fine in a few days," she assured him. "He must have picked up a flu bug at church last Sunday. That's the only place he's been to catch something."

"Poor kid. It was probably a shock to his immune system after not going anywhere all winter."

"Mmm hmm," Jenny agreed, piling dishes in the sink.

"Why don't you stay inside this afternoon and look after him. I can handle cleaning the barn by myself," Mike said, reaching for his coat.

"Thank you. I just hope you don't end up catching whatever he's got."

"I wouldn't worry too much about it," Mike said, and he headed for the barn.

"I'm not the one that has to worry," Jenny returned

with a smile as the door slammed behind him.

Filled with mixed emotions, she sank down in a chair and gazed at the door.

When had this happened? When had she fallen in love with Mike? Sometime between December and April, her heart had healed and learned to love again. But how? She didn't know. This love for Mike had come as softly and quietly as spring, remaining hidden until one day it blossomed.

"Lord, I don't know what to do. Please help me. You know my heart; You know my mind. Just tell me where to go from here, please."

At that moment the phone rang.

Jenny finished her short prayer. "Thank you, Lord. Amen."

She picked up the receiver. "Hello?"

"Hi, Jenny! How are you?"

"Laurie! You're just the person I've been wanting to talk to."

"It's nice to be wanted," Laurie said. "What's on your mind?"

"I ... just need to talk to someone."

"What, Mike's ears froze off in the last storm?"

"Not exactly. It's just ... he's what I want to talk about."

"Can you wait until Friday?"

"What do you mean?"

"I called to ask if you'd like to come with me to

The Bargain

Scottsbluff on Friday to buy groceries. Mike could look after Peter, and Frank's going to watch our boys. We could have a day on the town. What do you think?"

"I'd love to, if Peter feels better by then."

"What do you mean by if Peter feels better?"

"It's nothing serious, just a touch of flu, I think."

"OK. I'll plan to see you Friday."

Friday morning dawned clear and bright, promising warmth. The early morning was cold yet, with fog rising from the lake and pushing into corners of the valley. Jenny pulled a warm jacket out of the closet and glanced in the mirror one last time before going downstairs. Laurie should be here soon.

Mike and Peter were finishing their breakfast. They looked up when she entered the room. Mike whistled appreciatively, and Peter grinned.

"Wow, Mommy!"

She had French-braided her hair for the first time in months. A simple white blouse with daintily gathered sleeves and embroidered cuffs and collar was tucked into her new blue jeans, forming her "going to town" outfit.

"So, I pass inspection?" Jenny asked with a smile. Her cheeks were flushed, and her eyes sparkled in merriment. "Thank you."

Jenny reached over and kissed Peter on the cheek. "Behave for Mike, OK?

"There's potato salad and hamburger in the fridge and chocolate cake and cookies on the counter, so you won't starve. You can open a can of pork and beans if you want to."

They heard a pickup pull into the yard, and a horn honk.

"There's your ride. Go, and don't worry about us," Mike said, as Jenny pulled a can of beans from the cupboard. "Have fun."

"All right. Take care, you two," she said, grabbing her purse and a big ice chest before hurrying outside.

Jenny tossed the ice chest in the back of the pickup, hopped in the cab and shut her door.

"Ready to go?" Laurie asked.

"I hope so."

"I know. I checked three times to make sure the stove was off, and I'm still not sure it is." Laurie grinned, backing the pickup out of the drive.

"Mmm hmm." Jenny nodded, buckling her seat belt.

"Have you got your list?"

"Yep. Couldn't forget that."

Talk turned to where they needed to go when they got to town, and they were on the highway before there was a lull in conversation.

Laurie glanced over at her petite friend, wondering if Jenny would continue the conversation she had started on the phone Monday. She soon got her answer.

"Laurie?"

"Hmm?"

"Can I ask your advice on something?"

"Of course."

Jenny bit her lip, then said slowly, "What would you say if someone – someone lost someone they loved very much and thought they could never love again, but found that they could? Would it be wrong?"

"What are you asking?"

"When I lost David, I knew I would never love anyone again like I had loved him. When I first came here, I still grieved as though it had been just a few days since he died. But something has happened, and all of a sudden, I discover I love Mike.

"At first, he was a shoulder to cry on. Then he became a friend, someone I could talk to about anything. Now I wake up in the morning, and my first thought of the day is: I love Mike. How can that happen?"

Laurie thought her heart would break at the confusion she heard in her friend's voice. She carefully thought out her next words.

"Jenny, I don't claim to be an expert, but as a Christian, and as your friend, I'll give you my honest opinion. OK?"

Jenny nodded, and Laurie continued.

"When I think about losing Frank, I just want to curl up and die inside. I can't even imagine what you went through when you lost David. But I know it must have hurt you very much. Still, you've told me David was a Christian, and knowing that, you don't have the worry that you will never see him again. You'll meet again when this life is through.

"God doesn't want us to worship the dead and place them on a pedestal that towers above us. He too mourns the loss of one of His children, but He rejoices with them in heaven. That's the way it should be. Do you understand?"

Jenny nodded again.

"Saying that, I want you to know that I think it's wonderful that you have found love with Mike."

"But ... how could it just happen? Sometime in the last few months, I fell in love with Mike. How could I just forget about David like that?"

"Jenny, you didn't forget about David. You'll never forget him. He was a very special part of your life, and a part of him will always be with you.

"Maybe it was just time to move on, and you did. You're a beautiful young woman with a very long life ahead of you. You could have another wonderful marriage and maybe half a dozen children. Your life didn't end when you lost David, as much as you might have thought so at the time. It just kept going, and when it was time to move on, you did."

"How did you know just the right thing to say?" Jenny asked with a smile. "I don't feel guilty when you put it like that."

"You shouldn't. Loving Mike is nothing to feel guilty about. He's a wonderful guy with a heart of gold."

"Yes, but does he love me?"

"I don't know, but he'd have to be dead not to."

Jenny ignored that sharp remark. "To him, I'm just a friend."

"Maybe he treats you like that because he thinks that's how you want to be treated. If he knew how you felt, maybe you'd find he feels the same."

"Laurie, I just found out it was all right to love him. Now I have to tell the world how I feel?"

"Not the world, just Mike." Laurie laughed. "I'm not telling you to do anything. It's your decision. I'm just making a suggestion, that's all. It's up to you how you handle it. If you truly love him, go for it."

Jenny nodded and sank back against the seat. How was she going to tell Mike without knowing how he felt? There had to be a way that would keep her heart from getting broken. Maybe she should pray about it.

An hour later they arrived in town. Scottsbluff was bigger than Ogallala and had a mall and several large discount stores. Laurie stopped first at a farm and ranch supply store to buy a part for Frank. Then they drove to the mall. A few stores later, Laurie had found out two things: Jenny loved to read, and her birthday was May 20.

When Jenny wasn't looking, Laurie picked out a new book and a card that seemed perfect for the occasion. They went to lunch, then dug out their grocery lists and headed to the store. They were both tired when they started the long ride home at four o'clock.

Three hours later, Jenny was very glad to be home. Mike came out to help her haul the groceries inside. Welcomed by the warm, yellow lights and the smell of supper cooking, Jenny felt that, indeed, the world had no better place to offer than the one she called home.

Chapter 17

Love was so easy in the fairy tales, Jenny thought as she shut the book gently. Peter had fallen asleep sometime before "and they lived happily ever after." It had been a long day. Peter had attended his first branding today, and he was as worn out as she was.

Kissing him, she tucked the quilt up under his chin and quietly left the room, turning the light out as she went. As tired as she was, she wasn't ready for sleep just yet. She returned the book to a shelf in the den, chose another one and curled up in the big chair. Maybe if she read a few chapters she would feel ready to go to bed.

Mike sat in his chair and stared at the opposite wall. The house was too still, too silent. It was after nine o'clock, and he was still up. If he wanted to get up early tomorrow, he'd better get to bed. Still, he sat. There was a bigger problem weighing on him now. He was facing something that seemed to bring all the stark loneliness of his life into light, and he didn't like what he saw.

In a few days, they would be done feeding the cattle. He usually looked forward to the end of feeding, but not this year. Every other year, the end of feeding meant spring was finally here. This year, however, it meant much more. This year it meant the end of the bargain that had allowed him to see Jenny and Peter every single day since October. The bargain had allowed him to know what he was missing by not having a family. In a way, it had given him a family.

Soon Jenny and Peter wouldn't need his help on a daily basis. Mike felt the pain of missing them already.

Would he ever have Peter fall asleep on his shoulder again, trusting Mike to keep the world at bay? Would he remain a part of Peter's life as the boy continued to grow up? Or would he miss everything?

Mike realized with a start that he was thinking of Peter the way a father thinks of his son. Peter had shown him the joy of children, and the love a parent felt.

What he could not fathom, however, was the thought that he would not see Jenny. He had never experienced love like the love he felt for her. And he would never feel it again if he lost her.

He couldn't let her go, but he didn't know what to do. What if she didn't see him as anything more than a friend and he ruined even that by saying something?

"God, what can I do? Should I wait and see what happens?"

Go. The word came out of nowhere.

"Go? Go where?"

Go see her. Tell her how you feel. You'll never know unless you go.

"Now?"

Yes, now.

Mike got out of his chair wondering if he had been imagining things. Jenny was probably sound asleep in bed by now. Well, if there weren't any lights on, he would just have to wait until tomorrow. He was not getting her out of bed to make a fool of himself.

Mike grabbed a jacket and reached for the door, then changed his mind. He went into the bedroom, opened the top dresser drawer and removed the small box he had gotten in town before Christmas. Tucking it into his shirt pocket, he buttoned the flap tightly and hurried to the front door again. Nine-thirty already. It would be a miracle if she were still up. Well, God had been known to make miracles happen.

Jenny couldn't seem to lose herself in the book, as interesting as it might have been at another time. Dropping it in the chair, she went to the kitchen and mixed a glass of chocolate milk. Sipping it slowly, she doodled on the pad of sticky notes she kept on the counter. It was amazing how well Mike's name looked beside hers.

Headlights suddenly arced through the kitchen window. Jenny was alarmed. Who could be here at this time of night? There was a gentle knock on the door, and she hurried to answer it.

Pulling the door open, she saw with relief that it was Mike standing on the step.

"Hi," he said hesitantly.

"Hi. Is something wrong?"

"No. Nothing. I just – just wondered if you'd want to go for a walk?"

"A walk?" She looked out at the warm spring night and then at Mike.

"A walk sounds good. Just let me get a jacket." She took her hooded sweater from the coat rack and stepped outside, slipping her arms into the sleeves.

"It's beautiful out here," she said softly, looking up at the night sky as they began walking toward the meadow.

A hundred thousand stars shone brightly down on them, and a gentle breeze blew.

"Prettiest place in the world tonight," Mike agreed, looking up.

"I could get lost just looking at it," Jenny whispered, her head bent back in awe.

Her foot hit a stone, and she stumbled. Mike's fingers

twined around hers, and he laughed softly.

"I'd better hold on or you'll fly away."

She looked over at him, then around at the quiet meadow. From the lake came the soft call of a bird, settling down for the night. Wind whispered through the willow trees nearby. It was a comforting rustle. The air was clear and clean, scented with grass and earthy smells. They walked on in silence, reaching the narrow land bridge between the two lakes. There they stopped, and Mike turned to face her.

"Jenny, you're probably wondering why I came tonight. Well, there's something I want to tell you."

She looked at him, seeing her reflection in his dark eyes.

"Jenny, I've tried bein' your friend these past few months, but I don't think I can do it any longer."

She glanced down, her heart plummeting to her feet like a cold rock.

"I – I understand, if you don't want to see us anymore ... I –"

Mike dropped a finger to her lips, stopping her speech.

"No, no. I meant ... Jenny, I love you. You're the best thing that has ever walked into my life. If I have to face every day without you and Peter, life won't be worth living. I ... if you can't find it in your heart to love me, I'll still be your friend, but, Jenny, I – I love you. I want more than just friendship."

"I love you, too." She said it so softly he almost missed it. Then she repeated herself, louder, "I love you."

At this, her arms twined around his neck, and he kissed her. Moments later, Mike held her close and brushed his fingers across her face.

"You're crying." The tender concern in his voice made her smile.

"It's just ... I've been such a fool. I thought that you ... that you saw me only as a friend and that you could never love me. And now I find out that you've loved me all along."

"I couldn't help it."

"I'm glad," Jenny said before he kissed her again.

"I'm glad too. Now, how about a birthday gift, a little early?"

"What could you possibly give me that I don't already have right here?"

"You'll see."

He unbuttoned his shirt pocket and brought out the small box. She took it and slowly opened it, looking in wonder from it to him.

"Mike, what ..."

"Shh." Mike took the box from her grasp and removed a narrow gold band with a marquis diamond that gleamed in the moonlight.

"Jenny Cook, will you marry me?"

"Yes!" She shouted joyfully as he slipped the ring on

her left hand.

The stars, following their ancient course across the velvet sky, winked silently down at the couple. Somewhere a coyote howled, and the night wind blew colder, but nothing shattered the moment. No night was too dark where there was love. Had not the world and all the stars above been created by a loving God?

Jenny hummed happily as she beat eggs into the pancake batter the next morning. She heard a knock on the door, and Mike came in wearing a smile so wide it matched her own.

"Good morning!" He dropped a kiss on her lips and peered over her shoulder at the mixture in the bowl. "Pancakes?"

"Mmm hmm."

"Pancakes are good."

"I know. Especially blueberry pancakes." Jenny laughed.

"Sounds like a winner," Mike said with satisfaction.

"Like you have a choice!"

Mike laughed with her at that, eyes sparkling.

"I've been thinking," Mike began.

"Oh?"

"We ought to tell Peter about – about getting married and ask what he thinks. This is going to affect him just as much as us."

"Well, we can tell him this morning, but I don't think it will be a problem," Jenny said.

Mike didn't have time to reply. Peter bounced into the room, a shoe in hand.

"Mornin', Mike, mornin', Mommy!"

"Good morning!" Jenny said, as Peter pulled out a chair and crawled up to the table.

"How you doin', Peter?" Mike asked.

"Good. Can we go ridin' today?"

"Maybe."

"Yeah!" Maybe was almost as good as yes.

Mike changed the subject. "Peter, your mom and I want to talk to you about something."

"What?"

Jenny turned from the cupboard and faced the table. "Peter, what would you say if Mike married Mommy?"

"You mean like ... be a family?"

"Yes, like a family. Mike would live here with us. Would you like that?"

"How come?"

"I love your mom," Mike said, "and she loves me. And most of all, we both love you."

"Would you be my daddy?"

"If you want me to."

"Yes!" Peter shouted. "Yes!"

Jenny grinned at Mike. "It's unanimous. You're stuck with us."

"Yippee!" Mike yelled. Peter joined in, and Jenny retreated to the stove.

God had given her so much. How could she have known when she asked for somewhere to go that He would give her this and lead her to Mike? It was almost too much to take in. As she poured the batter for the first pancake on the hot griddle, she said a prayer of thanks. Then she joined in the merrymaking with a heart full of love and joy. She was truly blessed.

Chapter 18

"This is the first time I've heard of a potluck wedding dinner," Laurie said from the table where she was chopping onions.

"First time for everything. Besides, who wants to spend the day of the wedding cooking?" Jill replied, snitching a bite of onion as she added a pile of olives to Laurie's cutting board.

Jenny smiled at the rapport between her friend and soon to be sister-in-law. Jill and Laurie were enough alike to be sisters, both in manner and looks. Tall, almost lanky, both had the flawless polish of true platinum blondes, and both had a sharp wit that came out most when they were together.

The shrieks and laughter of four small boys and two little girls drifted through the open windows. Jill's husband, Brian, was outside taking his turn as chief baby sitter. Mike and his father had been sent to town for the flowers for tomorrow's wedding.

"Jenny, do you have a needle and thread? Beth's dress is too long."

"Of course, Karen." Jenny smiled at Mike's mother. As petite and dark as her daughter was tall and light, she was warm, friendly. Both Jenny and Peter had fallen in love with her instantly.

"Wonderful!" Karen beamed, turning to follow Jenny upstairs.

In the big closet, Jenny unearthed her grandmother's sewing box, and Karen went off to find the dress and little Beth to see just how much to adjust the hem.

Jenny stood a moment in the hall, letting the past few weeks catch up with her.

The wedding date had been set for June 20, tomorrow. She had wanted to be married here, and Mike had agreed. The wedding would be held outside on the lawn, under the trees, and each guest would bring a covered dish. It would be a Western wedding – fun, informal, and totally different from anything Jenny had ever imagined.

A week ago, Mike's family had arrived to help with the preparations, and ever since then, the big house had been full, pleasantly bursting at the seams. Jenny had insisted that Brian and Jill stay with her, since Mike's parents were staying with him in his small house. She had sorted through the belongings in her grandfather's room a few weeks ago, making it a guest room. Now it held Emily and Beth, Jill's and Brian's daughters. Jill and Brian were in Peter's room, and Peter had moved in with her.

"One big happy family," Jill had said this morning as they crowded around the breakfast table.

And they were – most of the time, Jenny thought.

A wail filled the air.

Hurrying downstairs, she saw little Joel sitting on Laurie's lap, explaining through his tears that "No one plays wid me!"

"You'll just have to help Mom then," Laurie announced, wiping tears from his eyes.

"No!" He shouted, crawling off her lap. "Don' wanna."

"Suit yourself." Laurie shrugged, and he stalked stubbornly out of the kitchen.

"I can pay wid that girl," Joel muttered as he left.

"A girl beats Mom all to pieces." Laurie laughed as the screen door slammed.

"It sounds like Brian's got him now," Jill said, peering out the window. "I think they're playing drop the hankie or something like that."

"Good. Now where's the macaroni? I need to mix this salad together so it can get cold."

"Is this for tomorrow?" Jenny asked, handing her a bowl from the refrigerator.

"This? Nope. We're just making supper."

"We're thinking of grilled hamburgers and hot dogs, macaroni salad, fruit salad, and ice cream. What do you think?" Jill asked.

"I think you ladies have everything under control."

Jenny grinned.

"You do, do you? Wait until you see what kind of a mess we're cooking up for tomorrow," Laurie threatened, flourishing a spoon.

"As long as you're helping, I'll let you make whatever mess you want."

After supper, Mike and Jenny found a moment to themselves. Leaving the others on the front porch, they walked west, holding hands and talking. The sun was dropping toward the horizon and the air was cool.

"Are you ready for tomorrow?" Mike asked.

"Oh yes. Very surely ready."

"I love you, Jenny Marie Cook."

"Then you don't have anything to worry about," Jenny said with a smile, "because I love you too."

As the sun dropped low, they returned to the house. After kissing Jenny good night, Mike collected his parents and drove home. Tomorrow she would be his wife. Tomorrow he would never have to leave her again.

"You're beautiful, my dear," Karen said, stepping back and looking Jenny up and down.

"Thank you." Jenny smoothed the skirt and looked in

the mirror on the closet door. The fitted bodice of her soft muslin dress had a sweetheart neckline. The front waistline dipped in a vee, and the skirt was full, falling to the floor. Karen had worked wonders with Jenny's hair, pulling it up into a French twist and adding the pearled comb Grandpa Riley had bought Grandma for their wedding.

A knock came at the door, and Jill entered, Beth and Emily behind her. The two girls wore matching calico dresses with lacy, white pinafores. Jill had not dressed yet. She was still in the jeans and T-shirt she had worn when she helped cook breakfast.

"Oh, Jenny! My dear brother is going to drop dead in his tracks when he sees you!"

"I don't think so, but Jenny is a beautiful bride, isn't she? Now what did you need, dear?" Karen asked.

Jill held a hairbrush in her hand. "I can't get Beth's hair to do anything, Mom."

"Let me try." Karen took the comb and pulled Beth over to the bed. One thumb in her mouth, the other hand clenching the skirt of her dress, the little girl did not take her eyes off Jenny.

Little Emily pulled her soon-to-be cousin Peter into the room and proceeded to comb his hair, fix his tie and tie his shoes with a very motherly air.

"There. That ought to look OK, don't you think, Aunt Jenny?"

"Mommy, I can't breathe!" Peter gasped.

The Bargain

Jenny knelt on the floor mindless of her dress and loosened the string tie. In black jeans and a black vest over a white Western shirt, Peter looked as though he had stepped out of the Old West.

"There. You're very handsome," Jenny said with a smile.

"Thanks, Mommy. When's the weddin'?"

She looked around at the clock behind her. "In about twenty-five minutes."

"Oh my goodness!" Jill cried. "I haven't even dressed!"

The house became a flurry of activity. Twenty minutes later, when everyone had gathered in the living room, Jill was picture perfect. Brian had kept Peter, Emily and Beth out of the way and clean, and now he had them gathered around with everyone else. Mike and his father, Dale, had arrived moments before, completing the group.

"It's almost time," Brian said, glancing at his watch. "Dad, would you lead us in prayer?"

Joining hands, they all bowed their heads as Dale began in his deep voice, "Father, today we will be welcoming two new members into our family. But in our hearts, they have already become a part of our lives. Thank you, Lord, for bringing us this new daughter and grandson. Lord, please be with Mike and Jenny as they begin their new life together. Watch over them through the good times, strengthen them in the bad, and love them always. Bless them as they travel through life together and keep them safe in Your love. In Your name, Amen."

Only the children did not have tears in their eyes when he finished. Jenny hugged her soon-to-be father-in-law.

"All right!" Karen clapped her hands together. "We have a wedding about to start! Places, everyone!"

The family scattered, and soon only Jenny and Dale remained inside. Outside, the murmur of voices drifted through the air. Their church family and many of their close neighbors had been invited to the wedding. They filled the folding chairs that the men had arranged on the lawn. The sound of music filled the air.

"It's time. Are you ready, daughter?" Dale asked.

Jenny looked at the tall old man with the gentle brown eyes so like Mike's and nodded, grasping the bouquet of sweetheart roses tightly. "Yes."

He opened the front door and offered her his arm. Together, they stepped onto the porch and started down the stairs.

The June sky was a perfect blue with tiny puffs of clouds sailing across it. The trees whispered in the breath of wind, and Jenny thought she had never seen a more beautiful day than today. Between the two great trees at the end of the sidewalk, Mike waited with Peter, his eyes upon her. The minister was beaming as he faced them, and Jenny smiled back. Laurie stood nearby, strumming her guitar in harmony with the gray-haired gentleman from church who was playing the violin.

Psalm 126:6 came to mind, and Jenny smiled, repeating the now familiar words in her heart. "He who goes out weeping, carrying seeds to sow, will return with songs of joy, carrying sheaves with him."

Inside she was calm, feeling a peace she had not known existed. This was her life – surrounded by friends and loved ones, the green hills across the valley, the sparkling blue of the lake, the birds in the nearby trees. She could not imagine a more wonderful place in the world.

They reached the minister, and Dale released her, finding a seat near Karen in the front row. The ceremony began, and before she knew it, they had repeated their vows and Mike was slipping the ring on her finger, looking at her with eyes full of love.

"I do."

"I now pronounce you man and wife," the minister said. "Mike, you may kiss the bride."

Her arms twined round Mike's neck, and as his lips touched hers, she knew that this was one bargain that would remain sealed for life.

Jo Maseberg was raised on a ranch in western Nebraska where she heard tales of the Old West and wrote cowboy poetry about her experiences in the new West. She currently lives in Kansas and finds time to write between attending classes at Ft. Hays State University and working. In her spare time, Jo enjoys doing research for future stories and hiking.

Fireside Library

Other books by OGDEN PUBLICATIONS

These Lonesome Hills	Letha Boyer
Home in the Hills	Letha Boyer
Of These Contented Hills	Letha Boyer
The Talking Hills	Letha Boyer
Born Tall	Garnet Tien
The Turning Wheel	Garnet Tien
The Farm	LaNelle Dickinson Kearney
The Family	LaNelle Dickinson Kearney
Lizzy Ida's Luxury	Zoe Rexroad
Lizzy Ida's Tennessee Troubles	Zoe Rexroad
Lizzy Ida's Mail Order Grandma	Zoe Rexroad
Many to the Rescue	Zoe Rexroad
Carpenter's Cabin	Cleoral Lovell
Quest of the Shepherd's Son	Jaunita Killough Urbach
Martin's Nest	Ellie Watson McMasters
Third Time for Charm	Mabel Killian
To Marry a Stranger	Glenda McRae
Pledges in the West	Glenda McRae
Sod Schoolhouse	Courtner King and Bonnie Bess Worline
Texas Wildflower	Debra Hall
River Run to Texas	George Chaffee
Home on the Trail	Mona Exinger
Horseshoe Creek	C.P. Sargent
The Longing of the Day	Louise Lenahan Wallace
Dr. Julie's Apprentice	Don White

Ogden Publications wishes to acknowledge the following for their efforts in the publication of this book: Ann Crahan, Cheryl Ptacek, Traci Smith, Diane Rader, Jean Teller and Vicki Schalansky.